NEVER DEAD

NEVER DEAD

WELCOME TO DEAD HOUSE™ BOOK ONE

M.L. BULLOCK

DISRUPTIVE IMAGINATION

Copyright © 2020 Monica L. Bullock
Cover by Fantasy Book Design
Cover copyright © LMBPN Publishing

LMBPN Publishing
PMB 196, 2540 South Maryland Pkwy
Las Vegas, NV 89109

First US Edition April, 2020
eBook ISBN: 978-1-64202-827-0
Print ISBN: 978-1-64202-828-7

Thank you to Michael Anderle and the LMBPN crew. This one's for you!

THE NEVER DEAD TEAM

Thanks to our Beta Team:
Micky Cocker, Theresa Holmes, Jim Caplan, John
Ashmore, Kelly O'Donnell, Rachel Beckford, Mary Morris

Thanks to the JIT Readers

Veronica Stephan-Miller
Deb Mader
Kathleen Fettig
Debi Sateren
Peter Manis
Dave Hicks
Jeff Goode
Diane L. Smith
Dorothy Lloyd
John Raisor
Angel LaVey
Micky Cocker
Paul Westman

If I've missed anyone, please let me know!

Editor
Lynne Stiegler

TAMARA

The aroma of French Roast coffee summoned me to the kitchen earlier than I planned. Luckily for me, Chloe could make her own breakfast and see herself off to school. I'd had every intention of sleeping until eight, but I was a sucker for a good cup of coffee and I couldn't help myself. I wouldn't accomplish anything hanging out in my comfy, albeit sometimes lonely bed. The bed was new, even if I couldn't say that for the rest of the furniture in the big old house. It was our house though, and come hell or high water, I was going to keep it for Chloe. I had promised her mom.

What was my plan after? I couldn't really say. I've always been one to wander. To check out the next town and get the vibe. Strangely enough, this crumbling plantation felt like home. Maybe I was just getting old, I groaned inwardly.

Shut up, Tamara. Coffee. Go get coffee.

Slipping on my fuzzy, pink slippers, I tried to arrange a

messy bun as I stumbled down the hall to the kitchen to fetch that first cup.

It would be the first of many, I predicted.

Late nights watching Ghost Hunters with Joey were beginning to take a toll on me. The episodes were all reruns, but I liked watching them because Joey enjoyed them so much.

Watching the shows made me nostalgic for the old days. Chloe's mom and I used to be into all that stuff. It was our practice to tour haunted locations with paranormal groups between gigs. I was more into the paranormal than she had been, but we had both been huge ghost fangirls.

To think she'd owned a haunted house all that time and never told me. Best friend, my ass. I would never understand, but it was water under the bridge now. The shock had worn off a bit of me being a proxy mom. Who'd a thunk it? But if it hadn't been for those excursions, I wouldn't have been prepared for what was happening here at Ridaught Plantation.

From day one, we had weird encounters, but Joey, the resident ghost, was harmless if a bit dramatic at times. We'd gotten along almost right away, but Chloe had a cool disdain for him. Exhausted the first night, I'd tossed sofa cushions on the floor and made a pallet for myself to collapse on after a day of moving. I woke up to the sound of someone rummaging through my hanging clothes.

The first few seconds of our encounter had terrified me, but Joey's relaxed demeanor quickly put me at ease. I went back to sleep and woke up believing it was all a dream. Nope. He rearranged my vanity table and my shoe rack a few days later.

Joey slipped into Chloe's room once to "help her get organized," but the teenager let him know quick, fast, and in a hurry it wasn't cool, a rule I adhered to as well.

I'd taken a day off from the usual hustle and grind of trying to sell houses to a disinterested local marketplace. I didn't have any connections in the cliquey town, and the locals were suspicious of anyone they didn't know. They sure as hell didn't know me, but I could be charming when I wanted to.

I was about to unleash the magic and pour it out in barrels if necessary. I'd be sweeter than syrup if it meant gaining the trust of a few influential neighbors. Sure, that cop Deputy Kevin Whatever-His-Last-Name-Was didn't trust me, but he was a red-blooded American male. Roll through one stop sign, and you're considered a criminal apparently. He'd change his mind eventually. I could still rock a pair of high heels.

I yawned and stretched my back as I continued the long walk to the kitchen.

Yep, I had to break into this local market and sooner rather than later if I wanted to keep the lights on. I wasn't one for rustic living.

That was the whole reason for hosting a Halloween party. From a marketing standpoint, it seemed a great idea. I'd even gotten Chloe on board with it. Opening the Ridaught Plantation to the community and letting them get a peek inside would be an excellent way for the local folks to get to know me. The historic home had been closed for a long time and people were naturally curious about it.

It couldn't hurt, could it? They didn't have to know everything about me.

If things didn't improve soon, financially speaking, I'd have to get a second gig, but doing what I had no idea. I'd kind of aged out on the whole burlesque deal. Clubs didn't want to bring in thirty-year-old performers when they had a constant stream of "fresher," aka younger acts to choose from. I could always hit the webcam highway.

Get over it, girl. You had your time in the limelight. You can do this without all that.

I rubbed my eyes and refused to look at my reflection in the dirty hallway mirror.

It would be great if my book actually took off. That was the plan, finish the book and maybe sell a few houses along the way. At least one, damn it. Today would get me one step closer to what I wanted. I was setting up my writing space. No more crummy desk in the corner of the bedroom. If I was going to take a real stab at becoming the next Anne Rice, I'd need to have a dedicated office. I'd already picked out which room I wanted to use and even the paint color for the walls.

I could hear Chloe's phone dinging away in the kitchen. I grunted as I joined her. She was pouring herself a to-go cup of coffee and loading it with sugar and milk.

See, Tina Louise? See how great I am at this whole parenting thing? I've taught your daughter how to make the breakfast of champions, caffeinated sugar juice, I thought. You're welcome.

There was no need to flick on the light because the kitchen had no curtains. I'd removed the broken blinds the first week we got here and hadn't replaced them yet. From my perfect view of the side yard, I could see gray, leafless trees and an overgrown lawn. Was it possible we'd been here a month already?

My, how time flies.

Sunlight streamed in over the sink and reminded me the dingy floors needed mopping.

Not today, Satan. I'm not mopping floors today. This is my day.

Chloe didn't bother saying good morning. Instead, she handed me a coffee cup and jerked her head toward the stove. "Why does the ghost have his head in the oven?" I groaned at the sight of Joey's bony ass sticking out of the appliance. He hadn't even opened the door.

"Morning to you, too, Chloe. Why don't you ask him yourself? I just got here." I shrugged as I pondered the same thing. Whenever Joey got flustered about something, he forgot he could open doors and move things around. When he was happy, he walked around just like Chloe and me. Whatever was going on with him definitely had him stressed out if he had his head in the oven.

"No, thanks. I'm not the ghost whisperer. I'll leave that to you but remind him my room is off-limits. I'll know if he goes snooping around in there. I've got my breakfast, and my ride is on his way. I think I'll wait for him outside," she said as her blue-painted fingernails tapped on her phone screen. "Nobody wants to see this. Or you. You look like hell, Tam. Please ask the ghost to wait until I'm gone to kill himself from now on."

I ignored her request. "You're not taking the bus?" She'd been having some trouble on there, and I hated to hear it had gotten so bad she didn't want to ride it anymore.

"Bus kids suck. I'm tired of their smart comments about me living in a haunted house. And all the other stuff they say." She sipped her coffee and avoided eye contact. She'd been doing that a lot lately. We had moments when we connected, or so I thought, but not recently. "Don't make a big deal about it, Tamara."

Oh, so it's about me.

"Trey is picking me up."

"The kid from the video game store? That's cool. Wait, here's some money." I stepped over Joey's ghostly behind, still poking out of the closed oven. He was talking to himself like he was trying to muster the courage to actually do the deed. Whatever the deed was. You could never tell with Joey. I dug through my purse and grabbed my Hello Kitty pouch, quickly found a few wrinkled dollars, and shoved them in her hand.

"What do I need money for?"

"Gas. We pay our own way around here. With money. Nothing else." I smiled and pretended this was natural. Joey's ridiculous position, her taking alternative transportation to school, my...everything. This was life now. I felt sorry that her new family wasn't normal. She didn't refuse the cash. I imagined, and it probably was my imagination, that she smiled back momentarily.

"Thanks. I'll see you later."

"Later," I answered as she left the house. The screen door made a slapping sound behind her. I turned my attention to Joey as I poured black coffee into my favorite Hello Kitty mug. "What exactly are you doing?"

"You heard her," he answered, his voice reverberating in the closed oven door. "I'm going to end it all. I'm killing myself. Goodbye, cruel world! Now stand back so you don't get hurt!" He gasped and took a deep breath, and then a few more. "Where's the..."

"It's not going to work."

"Don't try and talk me out of it," he panted breathlessly. He was inhaling and exhaling like a crazy person. A crazy dead person.

"That's an electric oven, Joey."

"So?" Joey snapped as he arched his back deeper and wiggled his behind a little as he breathed in deeply again. I shook my head as I dumped three teaspoons of sugar in my coffee cup and sat down at the rickety kitchen table.

"The worst you could do would be to roast yourself to death. That sounds long and painful, and I'm sure that's not what you want. That's not a gas oven, Joey. You can keep your head in there until the cows come home and it won't make a difference. And there's one more thing," I said as he pulled his head out of the oven and gave me a dirty look.

"What's that?"

"I hate stating the obvious again, but you leave me no choice. You're already dead, Joey. You want to talk about it, or am I supposed to guess? I can't help you if you aren't honest with me."

"You heard that man last night. Death is merely a perception," he answered as he got up and dusted himself off. It was a weird thing to watch because everywhere he dusted, like the hem of his shirt or the top of his pants, got a little blurry like he was made of chalk or something. He did look a little faded this morning. Apparently, late nights binge-watching paranormal shows wasn't good for dead folks either. Something clearly had Joey vexed. I couldn't for the life of me figure it out with no information. He'd been fine when I went to bed. I'd even left the television on for him.

"It's too early for guessing games and I'm tired. Some of us didn't get our full eight hours of sleep. Living people need rest, you know," I complained as I sat crossed legged in the chair and waited for my coffee to cool.

"I can see that. What's this?" Joey asked as he hover-sat in the chair beside me. He was thumping his fingers between his eyes. "This. Are those wrinkles?"

"No," I told him defiantly. I rubbed the space between my eyes and frowned at him. "I slept hard is all. Give me a break, Joey, or I'm going to stick *my* head in the oven."

"Oh, that's not making it better. You should probably stop. Better hit that concealer, Tam. At least I'll never have wrinkles." He shivered as if just the thought of getting older gave him the willies.

"I hate you right now." I flipped him off to add extra meaning to my statement.

"You know who else has wrinkles?" A matching coffee cup manifested in front of him.

"I don't have wrinkles. I'm not there yet." I attempted to sip my coffee and avoided making eye contact with my ghostly best friend.

"Oh, you're such a bad liar, sweetie. Such a bad liar. Frowning, like this," he said as he waved his nearly translucent hand over my face, "makes those lines deeper."

"I see what you did there," I remarked before taking a sip of coffee. "Turning this around on me isn't going to distract me. We were talking about you slowly roasting yourself in the electric oven, remember? Maybe we should call Dr. Phil?"

"God forbid. His bald head would be too much of a distraction."

I took a big swig before continuing. "Jason's bald, and you love him."

"Jason?" Joey answered coyly.

"Yeah, Jason. Your favorite ghost hunter."

"Oh, he's not my favorite."

We sipped our coffee in silence. I wondered why he wanted to kill himself, and if that was how he'd died.

"What do they call those eye wrinkles? Crow's feet?" Before I could think of a witty comeback, his face suddenly went blank. "Uh-oh."

"Uh-oh, what?" I rubbed my forehead again. Was I growing a horn or something?

"You've got company, sweetie. Later. You might want to pass by a mirror before you open the front door."

"What?" Joey vanished in a tiny puff of smoke, and I was left alone in my kitchen. I got up from the table just in time to hear heavy knocking at the front door.

Great. I was a wrinkled train wreck and I had a visitor.

"Just a minute," I called, knowing good and well my visitor couldn't hear me. The front door was too far from the kitchen. "Shoot!" I left my cup behind and raced toward the bedroom to find a pair of shorts.

"I'm coming," I yelled as I hopped down the hall to greet my guest. Could it be the mailman? He didn't usually come this early and didn't typically knock. "Yes?" I asked as I swung open the large wooden door.

Deputy Kevin Patrick was standing on my front porch,

and naturally, he looked like he'd stepped out of GQ magazine, law enforcement edition. Damn. Did I have a warrant or something?

"Miss Garvey? Did I wake you up?"

No sense denying it when I looked like an unmade bed. "May I help you, Officer?" My sarcasm wasn't wasted on him.

"Deputy, not officer. I would think you would know that by now. What is this? Our third encounter?"

Encounter? Geesh. Did he think I was afraid of him? That Tamara Garvey was going to shake like a virgin on prom night at the mere sight of a cop standing on her porch? From his sullen expression, it was clear I was never going to live the stop sign incident down. Or the disturbance call from the grocery store. Have one argument with the cashier about accepting a check, and they call the law on you. The good deputy acted like I was a habitual offender. "I've lost count. What can I help you with, Deputy?"

"Just a welfare check. We got a call about a woman screaming. Are you okay? What about Chloe? Anyone else in the house?" I rubbed my eyes and considered inviting him in but decided against it. I didn't like the idea of Deputy Patrick having me at a disadvantage. I always got the feeling he wanted to slap those handcuffs on me, and not in a good way.

"I think someone is pranking you, Deputy. I've been here all morning. I didn't hear anyone screaming, and Chloe has left for school. I saw her five minutes ago. She barely said goodbye when she left." I frowned at him.

He raised his hand and radioed into his dispatcher.

"Resident says no. Are you sure it was coming from the Ridaught place?"

"Caller says yes."

Suddenly both of us heard it. A loud scream filled the air.

It was coming from upstairs.

2

ANNIE HENSLEY

1987

My white leather shoes made unsettling sticky noises as I traveled across the bare floor. There was a run in my tights and my arms were freezing. One of the disadvantages of wearing white to work every day was collecting stains. I would undoubtedly collect a few here if I continued on my search.

I usually wore a cardigan when I went out, but I'd left my sweater at the nurses' station. I was nowhere near the senior home, but instead, I'd broken into the deserted Ridaught Plantation in search of Marjorie Banks, my favorite but recently, most demanding resident. Going back without Marjorie wasn't an option, and I had an inkling she might be here. Marjorie couldn't drive, and she was barely mobile some days. Even walking had been a challenge lately, but this house cast a spell on sweet Marjorie.

I heard other footsteps walking across the gritty floor.

Maybe Marjorie had found her way over here. It had been her singular purpose for longer than I could remember. I'd always wanted to visit the deserted plantation, just for curiosity's sake, but this wasn't the way I imagined I'd take my maiden voyage.

There was no way Marjorie could be hiding here. How could an elderly woman cross acres of forested land and break into a boarded-up house? Okay, it hadn't been boarded up. The door had opened quite easily, but there was no way Marjorie could have traveled over hills and through woods by herself. She could barely find her way to the cafeteria on her good days.

I should have done as Marjorie asked and brought her here so she could see the place again one last time. Maybe then she would have let it go. Marjorie had been obsessed with the Ridaught family, as many people were in this neck of the woods. She was a Crystal Springs native and knew the grease on everyone from back in the day. It was heartbreaking to witness her deterioration.

I whispered into the husk of a home. "Marjorie? It's me. Annie. You're not in trouble, but I need you to come out, sweetie." I glanced at my watch. Nearly five o'clock. It would be dark soon.

I'd stumbled on this job after my failed relationship with Harry. Harry moved on in that big truck of his, the one I helped finance, but I didn't have the luxury of pouting about it. I had bills to pay and a life to live, and it didn't take long for me to fall in love with a few residents, including Marjorie. She used to tell me stories about the goings-on here. She was like family to me. The only family I had left.

Like many people at the home, Marjorie was losing her grip on reality. The disease was wreaking havoc on her memory and her vocal cords. She couldn't express how she felt, but I knew about her fixation on the Ridaught Plantation from before her diagnosis. We'd sit in the solarium together, and once in a while, she would say things like, "Did you see that, Annie? Do you see the lady in the window?" I would always say no, but in the back of my mind, I sometimes wondered if maybe Marjorie saw something I couldn't. Fringe magazines like the ones Harry used to read mentioned this sort of thing. One article said quite plainly that people with her type of disease develop other abilities as a kind of compensation. It wasn't a scientific diagnosis, but it brought me comfort.

I wanted to believe she was in that dainty head of hers. Somewhere.

"Marjorie? Marjorie, hon?" I whispered cautiously as I rubbed my arms, trying to warm them up. "Marjorie? It's time to go home. Please come out."

As I walked through the rooms, I realized how incredible a feat it would be for someone as frail as Marjorie to have made this journey by herself. Most of the time, she got about in a wheelchair I had to push, but sometimes she used a walker. There were rare days when she was very mobile and spirited and nonverbal. Her fixation with this house never wavered.

I never liked the look of this place. She'd sit in the solarium and stare, even though the view was obscured by dark green cedar trees and various and sundry other foliage. Marjorie would watch it as if it were the most interesting television program she'd ever seen. Now that she couldn't speak or verbalize what it was she saw, I worried about Marjorie and her continuing fascination with the Ridaught Plantation. I'd even made a call to her daughter, but she had not returned it. Nobody cared about Marjorie except me.

I stood in the center of the largest room, the floor beneath me black and white tiles, like an old-fashioned checkerboard. I didn't much care for the feeling in this room with its empty alcoves and bookshelves. They made it feel even more foreboding. Every step I took felt as if someone watched every move I made.

"Marjorie? Come out, please. We have to go home. It's getting late, and your daughter is going to be worried about you." I lied, but I was desperate. The only answer was the faint sound of footsteps. I couldn't tell if they were made by a human or an animal.

I paced across the room as I tried to locate the source. Then there was crying. Now, that was a cry I recognized. She was here!

Marjorie was here at the Ridaught Plantation!

Was she behind me? I retraced my steps back through the rooms I just passed through. There were a few scant pieces of furniture, and no curtains to hide behind. "Marjorie, where are you?" I listened as I prayed I would hear another clue. She had to be in trouble. She might be injured in some fashion.

Suddenly I was cloaked in shadow and there was nowhere to run.

3

TAMARA

Another scream echoed off the side of the porch, not as powerful or as loud as the one from upstairs. I felt like a cat caught between two rocking chairs. My neighbor, who I had only met on two previous occasions, zipped up the stairs toward us. She was sporting bright pink capris, a sleeveless shirt, and a visor, the kind you'd wear golfing or fishing. According to her equally bright pink tennis shoes, she'd been out walking.

"I heard the screams! Are you all right? Is it Chloe? Where's the ambulance?"

"We're fine," I said, wondering what the heck was going on. Who was screaming upstairs? Joey? He wouldn't dare do that to me.

"You ladies stay here!" The deputy raced into the house, practically shoving me to the floor as he ran to assess the situation. He cleared the foyer and bounded up the stairs in a matter of seconds. Out of the corner of my eye, I saw Joey hanging out in the hallway. He'd tucked a few pink curlers in his short hair and still held a coffee cup in his hand.

This ain't the time, Joey. You better not have anything to do with this.

If he could hear my mental message, he didn't let on. I don't know why he would. We didn't talk telepathically, or whatever you'd call that. Joey peeked up the stairs and then shrugged to show me had no idea what was happening. I couldn't help but shrug back to show him I had no idea either.

Linda, the neighbor, didn't seem to notice the exchange. "We better stay down here, Tammy. That scream sounds like someone is being tortured! Oh, God! It's terrible. I swunny, it does sound like someone is dying!"

"It's not Tammy. It's Tamara. Why don't you stay here? This is my house, and I'm going upstairs with the deputy. I'm sure others are coming. Why don't you keep an eye out for them?"

Linda gasped in shock. "You can't go up there! Didn't you hear those screams? I'm surprised the whole town didn't hear them. It sounds like someone is getting murdered." She shook her head and added in a whisper, "I wouldn't doubt it in this house, and it wouldn't be the first time."

"No one is getting murdered. I'm sure there's some explanation for all this. Just stay here."

Joey sipped from his ghostly cup of coffee and watched our exchange with some amusement. I tied my robe tightly around my waist and jogged up the first flight of stairs. As I cleared the first landing, Linda called from the porch. "Is it safe?"

"No, it's not. Stay there, Linda."

The last thing I needed was her footsteps stomping up behind me. My nerves were stretched like the strings of a guitar, an old guitar with even older strings. The hair on my neck was standing on end, and my stomach rumbled hungrily, but I didn't hear a thing upstairs.

"Officer? I mean, Deputy?" I whispered as I began climbing up the second flight of stairs. The treads were warped, and it probably wasn't safe to be moving too quickly. "Hey, can you hear me?"

"I hear you. In here." Deputy Patrick's voice echoed from one of the empty rooms down the hall on the left side. There were six rooms on the left and six on the right. As I started toward the sound of his voice, I felt a man's hand touch my elbow.

"Holy hell!" I screamed as I turned to see Deputy Patrick glaring down at me.

"What are you doing up here?"

"I thought you were down the hall. Weren't you…"

"I asked you to stay downstairs." The dark-haired law enforcement officer shoved his gun in his holster. "I didn't find anything on this floor. Do you have a key to the attic? It's locked. That's the only room I haven't cleared."

I snatched my arm away from him. "I was never given a key to the attic. I was told it was lost. I've got to have it rekeyed. Feel free to break it down if you feel you need to. Or maybe you could just blow a hole in it." I didn't mean to sound so testy, but I was on edge. "I heard a voice coming from that room. A man's voice, not a woman's. What the hell is going on up here?"

We hadn't gotten off on a good foot, and I can't say it

was entirely my fault. Who gives someone a ticket for rolling through a stop sign? I guess in his mind, I would always be a law-breaking so and so. I don't know why we had this distrust between us, but I wasn't eager to explore the reasons.

To my surprise, he took my hand, and together we went to the middle room. "You heard a voice in here?"

"Yes, that's right, I think. The voice sounded like yours. I'd swear it on a stack of bibles." I chewed a fingernail as I watched him go in. It couldn't be Joey. He'd never done anything like this. But if one ghost was here, others could be, theoretically speaking. Great, more dead people. Maybe a bunch. The thought sent another shiver through me.

The door was standing wide open, but there was no one in the room. I could see that from the doorway. Even the closet door stood open, and there wasn't a stick of furniture to hide behind.

"Nothing in here." Deputy Patrick stepped inside the closet and felt around with his hands. What was he looking for? Speaker wire? As if I'd resort to doing something shady like that. "Let's head back down and reassess the situation."

"Reassess? I don't understand any of this."

Linda and Joey were waiting for us, although Joey wasn't looking happy. He was mouthing something to me, but I wasn't great at lip-reading, and it wouldn't be a good idea to ask him directly. He'd just have to wait. He left the room with an exasperated sigh. I kept my eyes focused on the living.

"Aren't you having a party here in a few weeks? Some big Halloween fiesta?" Deputy Patrick asked as his shoulder-mounted radio squawked to life. A female dispatcher asked him a bunch of questions, but I couldn't interpret any of it. Clearly, a 10-3 or a 9-2 or whatever was cop code for, "This lady is full of crap."

I crossed my arms. "Fiesta? I've never hosted a fiesta in my life. For the record, I have no plans to broadcast screams to advertise my party, if that's what you're thinking. The only sounds coming from this place will be whatever the DJ plays."

He listened for a few seconds as he stared down at me. He tapped the radio. "Negative. All clear."

Linda watched the exchange in slack-jawed disbelief. "Well, I know what I heard. Could it have been a record player, Kevin?"

"I don't have a record player. Or a CD of a woman screaming."

The dark-haired deputy walked around the bottom floor for a few minutes while Linda eyed me suspiciously.

Great. This is just great.

"You didn't hear the other sounds?" Linda asked in a whisper when we were alone.

"What other sounds?"

Linda peeked into the other room and put her hand to her mouth. "While you were gone, I heard growling sounds, like the devil was walking around. I am really concerned about you and Zoe. "

"It's Chloe. There are no devils walking around here, except the one wearing a badge," I answered her as Kevin made his way back to us.

"I'm going to check the rest of the grounds. It would be

great if you could find the key to the attic while I'm gone." He gave me another stern look.

"As I said, I don't have a key to the attic. I never did. If you think I had something to do with this, you've got another think coming." No, that's not how that phrase went. Whatever. It was too damn early to be arguing with a cop and my intrusive neighbor.

Deputy Patrick didn't stick around to argue with me. He disappeared around the corner of the house while Linda hovered nearby. "You're so brave, living in this house. If you ever need my help, you just let me know."

"Help? What kind of help?"

"With psychic matters," she whispered through heavily lined and pink painted lips. "It's an open secret. My family says I have a gift. I see the dead all the time. In fact, I think I'm getting a message now." She closed her eyes and put her fingers to her temples as she concentrated on connecting with her imaginary ghosts. There was at least one ghost at the Ridaught Plantation, but she'd been standing next to Joey the whole time and hadn't known.

"Uh, thanks, Linda. I better go look for that key. Thanks for stopping by." I smiled as I walked to the front door and held it open. I heard Joey banging drawers in the kitchen and saw Linda's eyes perk up, but she didn't ask me about who else was here.

Come on, lady. Work with me here.

"Well, if you change your mind, remember I'm just next door. Stop in anytime."

"Thanks, Linda." Without too many more formalities, my nosy neighbor left me in peace, and the cop car soon followed. I watched him back out of the driveway slowly while hiding behind the flimsy lace curtains.

A crashing sound like a metal bomb going off drew my attention back to the kitchen.

"Now what?" I murmured as I huffed down the hallway. "Joey?"

4

KEVIN

"I'll be honest, she's got an attitude." I hoped that bit of information would end this line of questioning. "Garvey is spelled G-A-R-V-E-Y, right? Not double E? I did check for aliases the last time I met her, but you can spell Garvey a few ways."

Willie Mae pursed her lips thoughtfully. "Not that I can see, and I looked her up on Google. Are you sure you aren't spelling it Gravy?"

I tapped my pen on the desk and sighed. "No. Not Gravy. There's nothing under her name in the DMV database. No, Tamara Garvey."

"Did you ask her how to spell it or take a look at her license? Come to think of it, there should be a record of your ticket. Want me to call the DMV back? You know those gals and guys at the parish office aren't that hip with the technology."

"Don't do that. It must be a mistake. I'll be glad when they bring our records division up to twenty-first-century standards. She's not in there." Why was I feeling so damn grouchy? I couldn't shake the feeling that this Tamara Garvey, or whatever her name was, had a secret, one I needed to know.

"That doesn't explain who was doing all that screaming, Kevin. You said you heard it too, and it wasn't the Garvey woman." I rejected the older woman's attempt to come to some paranormal conclusion. She'd already mentioned "haunted" and "ghost" in our brief conversation several times. "They say Ridaught Plantation is a hundred percent haunted. Nobody has been brave enough to live there, much less go inside, and now she's having a Halloween party?"

"Come on, Willie. You're too smart for that."

She shrugged and pushed her glasses back on her nose. "Invited the whole town to her party from what I heard. I'm going as Dolly Parton, of course. What about you? I could use a Kenny Rogers sidekick."

I shook my head noncommittally. "I would never pass for Kenny Rogers. The screams were a prank, probably a recording or some weird-ass technology. Like a motion detector."

Willie nibbled at the end of her pencil. "A motion detector, but instead of a triggered light, it screams?"

"That's not what I mean. I checked the second floor, but there was no one up there. I couldn't get into the attic and poke around because she had it locked up—conveniently enough."

Willie said nervously, "Bad things happened in that attic, Kevin. I will tell you all about it sometime but not today. Heads up—the sheriff is in a foul mood. You be careful if you go back to the Ridaught place. Be really careful."

"I am always careful. If the scream wasn't coming from Miss Garvey, then it had to be something the teenager rigged up. Either way, I've got better things to do than deal with pranks," I announced as I scribbled on the report form. Filing a report for a prank was a ridiculous waste of time, but there was an election coming up, and I couldn't get away with skipping a single step in the investigation process. The sheriff wouldn't go for that.

"Chloe Carol is a good student, and she's at school. Remember? I called to confirm." Willie Mae frowned at me over her horn-rimmed glasses as she slid them back on. She glanced around the empty office and lowered her voice to a whisper. "If you ask me…" Before the ancient secretary and sometimes dispatcher could offer me further opinions, Sheriff Jarvis poked his sweaty head out of his office.

"Got a minute?"

"Yeah, sure," I said as I excused myself and hurried behind the short man and closed the door as he instructed me. That was pretty unusual as the sheriff and I didn't have too many closed-door meetings. There were only four of us on the police force, not including Willie Mae, but there was no doubt that this area of the county was growing, and eventually we would need a larger police force to serve and protect efficiently. Randy, the night shift patrol, told me a Smokey Joe's café was coming to town. It would be nice to have somewhere else to eat besides the usual fast food joints and Granny Brown's Country Kitchen.

"Have a seat, Deputy Patrick."

"Am I in trouble?" I asked uncomfortably. Sheriff Jarvis

wasn't usually this formal, and I couldn't fathom the need for a closed-door meeting.

"No, of course not. Unless you have something you need to confess. How did it go at the Ridaught place?" Sheriff Jarvis eyed me critically as he mopped his forehead with a flimsy handkerchief. Why was the man always sweating? It was freezing in his office.

"A prank is the likeliest scenario. The new resident is having a Halloween party, so it's probably just theatrics to garner some attention. She's a real estate agent and works for Royal Real Estate. I'm still working on it. What can I help you with, Sheriff?"

Jarvis leaned on his desk and folded his arms, a move that made him seem even smaller and more tired. "I'll cut to the chase. I need your help, Deputy, and in a big way. I want movement on the cold case situation. Put the Ridaught stuff to the side, we've got bigger fish to fry." He shoved a few dusty file folders in my direction with a stern look that encouraged me to accept them.

"Cold case situation? You want me to work on cold cases, Sheriff? What about the state's task force request? I'm the ranking officer here. I've got a meeting this Friday with Doug Hildebrand." I laughed, but it sounded dry and not genuine. How long had it been since I'd really had a good laugh?

"That meeting is off, at least for you. I'll handle that one, Deputy. I need you working these cold cases, and I mean working them hard. You need to trust me on this."

I flipped through the old folders and asked, "What's the rush?" That was a stupid question. It was election time in the county.

He didn't offer an answer. "I've selected three cases that are fairly recent to give you a better chance of success. I want, no, I need you to commit yourself to solve these cases. The one you're holding in particular, she was a nurse. Found dead near Estefan Creek. You've probably heard about the case. Annie Hensley. Died in 1987. That's far too long for a nice lady to go without justice. We need to close that one at least, but preferably all three if you can manage it. Get Willie Mae to do some research for you. She loves that stuff, you know, playing Nancy Drew."

Bewildered at this unexpected turn of events, I couldn't think of anything to say that didn't involve cuss words. The sheriff wasn't one for swearing.

"I'm sure you agree with me. Annie Hensley and these other two victims deserve justice."

I plopped the folders back on the desk. "That's not even a question, is it? Are you questioning whether or not I want justice for these people? What's going on here, Sheriff? Why am I being sidelined with cold cases?"

I'm not running for any damn election, I thought sourly but didn't say.

"Sidelined? This isn't sidelining you, Deputy Patrick. I'm giving you a chance to shine, and to stand out from the competition and believe me, there will be plenty of competition for this position, although I can't say why. It's a shit job with no praise and very little satisfaction."

"I'm not following you. What competition?"

The sheriff let out a deep sigh and wiped his face again. We'd known one another for a long time. I'd come to the force fresh out of the police academy, but the sheriff had always been a patient man. A good man, if not a little too eager to please the more prominent business folks in the community, not that I would ever believe he'd sell us out for a better parking spot or a few greenbacks. In the ten years I had worked in the county, we had never had a falling out. I didn't agree with all his decisions, but I trusted him to make good ones, at least until now. I was having one hell of a bad morning for damn sure.

"I don't plan on running for sheriff again, Patrick. Not this time. I'm out of the race for good. It's retirement for me. That's the plan. I've had a good run, but I've got to look after myself."

That got my attention. "What are you talking about, 'out of the race?'"

"I'm sick, Kevin. Sick in a bad way. The worst kind of way, but I'm not going to roll over and die, not yet. I feel like I'm half dead now. This medication has me sweating and heaving. I'd appreciate it if you would keep this to yourself. I don't want people asking a lot of questions, especially Willie Mae. You know she'd get all weepy-eyed. I don't need that kind of pressure. I've got to go to Birmingham for the rest of the treatments. I'm not going to have a lot of time to button things up here before I go, but these cases..." The sheriff began to cough, and I waited for him to get control of himself. "Sorry. Got a cold on top of everything else. If the Big C doesn't kill me, maybe the flu will."

"Come on, Sheriff. Don't say things like that. Do you mean the Big C as in..."

"Don't ask. It becomes real if you say it. Just know that I'm sick as hell. These cold cases, I can't go out without knowing I've done everything I can to help them. Annie Hensley deserves a fresh look, all of them do."

I couldn't hide my shock. This was not how I expected this conversation to go. "I'm really sorry, Sheriff. If there's anything I can do…"

"Don't wimp out on me, Deputy. This is the something you can do!" His fingers thumped the folders. "Solve these cases. Find out what happened to Annie and the others. I'm going to hold off on my recommendations to the mayor and the city council until I hear from you. Two weeks' time isn't much, but it's all I can give you, and in my mind, there's no one better for the job. You love Crystal Falls and this parish, that much I know. I should have put you on these before all this, but you know what they say." He smiled as beads of sweat reappeared on his forehead. His pause asked me to complete his sentence with the correct metaphor like I was some kind of mind reader. Reminded me of my dad when he did that, God rest his soul.

"Don't put the cart before the horse?"

The sheriff's smile vanished. He shook his head and waved his damp handkerchief at me. "Just go before I throw up on you. And remember to keep your mouth shut."

I tucked the folders under my arm and left his office. As soon as I stepped into the hallway, it came to me. "Hindsight is twenty/twenty."

"Finally got one," I heard him say before he started coughing again.

Willie Mae didn't ask me any questions as I settled down at my desk with the case files. She dabbed her dark cheeks with a tissue and clicked on her keyboard. I might have known she knew already. Willie Mae Fredericks knew everyone and everything.

Damn it all. This sucked.

With some effort, I put Tamara Garvey and her anonymous screamer out of my head and turned my attention to Annie Hensley. These past ten years, Sheriff Jarvis hadn't asked me for anything, not specifically, and certainly nothing as important as solving a cold case. He had often talked about how heartbreaking it had been to give up on finding Annie's killer. His boss closed the file but always kept it in his desk. I hadn't been around then, but I knew we didn't have the manpower to tackle a murder case in the eighties. We could hardly manage to navigate one today.

Murders don't happen in Crystal Springs. Not very often.

I would do this and not because Jarvis wanted me to become sheriff. I wasn't even sure I wanted to serve in that office. I was sure I wanted to make him proud and bring him some peace. He deserved that much from me.

I flipped the file open to the first page.

5

TAMARA

"Joey?" I stepped into the kitchen and nearly passed out. All the silverware, the good silverware collection I found here in the house, was stacked up on the breakfast table like a strange sculpture. I had never owned anything as nice as these silver utensils. Clearly, they were antiques of some value. Besides the silverware, the silver thimbles I'd found in the china cabinet drawer were clumped up along with the rest of it, and there was a silver cup I did not recognize. Where had that come from? This was the weirdest thing I had ever seen, and I was no stranger to weird. The arrangement wasn't merely stacked forks, but each fork rested at an angle, with knives poking up, and spoons too.

There was plenty of light, but I couldn't help myself. I flicked the switch to get a better look. "Joey? Did you do this? Cut it out!"

No answer.

I'd never known Joey to be a prankster. He would go for a laugh on occasion, but intentionally frighten me? Never. And I was dang terrified at the moment. The chairs weren't moved, the back door was securely locked, and there was no one else in this house.

Except whoever had been doing all the screaming earlier.

Now what? Did I call the effing cop back here to investigate this? Hell no.

"Hey? Don't hide from me, Joey." I slid open a few drawers, but all the cheap, everyday silverware was right where I left it. Only the real silver was utilized for this freak show. I opened the cabinets hoping Joey would pop out of one. Other than this morning's episode with the oven, I'd never seen him messing around in here too much. Keeping a careful eye on the stack, I opened another cabinet. Every dish and plate was where it should be. I walked around the table, amazed. If I bumped the table even slightly, I was sure it would all fall apart. I needed evidence of all this. I needed my phone. Or a camera.

The room got cold. Ice cold. I did what any sensible woman would do.

I backpedaled out of the room and turned off the light on my way.

"Joey!" I shouted as I raced back to my room, forgetting all about keeping the evidence intact. Time to get dressed and get out of the house for a while. I had to think this through before Chloe got home.

As soon as I hit the bedroom door, I gathered my senses. Back in the day, which really wasn't that long ago, I would have killed for an opportunity like this. Living in a haunted house and investigating the paranormal without restraints.

Why was I running?

I knew what to do and how to manage this situation. All those weekends with Tina Louise. All those weekends, bestie and you couldn't tell me about this place? I couldn't count how many sleepless nights I spent walking the halls of a lonely sanitarium, hoping to see my gadget's lights change colors. Or see anything at all.

Why were you hiding this place from me, Tina? Why leave it in my hands, and why would you want Chloe here?

As usual, all my questions remained unanswered, but I thought I could put an end to that if I put my mind to it. Tina Louise had to have left me some clues in this place, and here I was about to run in the opposite direction.

Nope. Wasn't going to happen. I had never been one to run, even when that rocking chair started moving at Waverly, or when the shadow followed us out of the Red Leaf Graveyard. Tina Louise had skedaddled, but not me. I'd sidestepped the path and let it pass me by, mesmerized by the sight.

I decided to put on some jeans and a clean t-shirt. As I got a handle on my breathing, I ran a comb through my hair and brushed my teeth. I dug into my very neatly organized closet, thanks to Joey, and found my camera. The first order of business was pictures and lots of them. Better to have two devices recording this in case one decided to die on me. Battery drain was no joke.

I couldn't do this on my own. I was definitely experiencing activity, and I still had ties to the paranormal community even though I hadn't been active for at least a year. I hadn't done any investigations since Tina Louise... Better to not go there.

I walked back to the kitchen and flicked the light on again. Everything was as I left it. I immediately took a variety of shots with the camera from all angles. When I was satisfied I had enough to document this strange occurrence, I pulled my phone out of my back pocket and snapped several bursts. Examining the table brought me no information. There were no magnets, and no devices, nothing to suggest any living person had a hand in this. At least I wasn't so damn terrified now, but I was puzzled and no closer to figuring out what happened.

Could Chloe have snuck in here and arranged the silver in such a complex formation, with no help, and no sound? I'd heard someone bumping around when Linda was dawdling in the foyer, but that was nowhere near long enough for Chloe or anyone else to do this kind of thing.

I headed to my office and powered up the computer. It only took a few tries to find pictures similar to mine. The paranormal activity in each instance was described as "poltergeist."

Great.

My mind couldn't help but go to the *Poltergeist* movie, only this was no movie. This was my life. I glanced at the clock. Chloe only had half a day of school today, because of some kind of teacher workday or whatever. That didn't leave me very long to disassemble that monstrosity before she got home. I couldn't leave it for her to see it. Talk about freaking her out.

I had plenty of photos, but I needed to take some video. Maybe do some EMF readings and try the K2. Where had I packed all those things? Out of the corner of my eye, I saw movement. I froze at my desk, clutching the mouse as if it were some sort of life preserver.

"Joey! Stop playing around!" I warned as I turned my head slowly in the direction of the open door. "Joey?"

Leaving the mouse on the desk, I walked into the hallway and looked around. There was nobody out here walking around wearing white. It had been a slim figure, moving fast, wearing a long white shirt or a dress. When had Joey ever worn white or a dress? Even when he was doing his weird fade in and out thing, he didn't look like a traditional white apparition. Joey always looked kind of natural, especially when he got stressed out as he'd been that morning. I never did get a straight answer from him. My interview had been cut short by our unexpected visitors. Another curious thing was how the neighbor lady heard the first scream, but neither Joey nor I did. The scream I heard sounded as if a woman were being murdered. If I had heard that, I would have been the one calling the police.

A strange tingling on my arm caused me to turn around. Did someone just touch me? This had happened earlier too, upstairs. That was not cool.

"Hey! Whoever you are, don't do that. You aren't allowed to touch me." My voice echoed back at me down the empty hallway. The fine hairs on my arms rose up as I heard a new sound. Footsteps, but not in this hallway, but above me. Was Deputy Patrick back?

As quietly as any herd of thundering elephants, I ran up the stairs and hung out in the hallway. No more footsteps. "Hey, I know you're here, idiot. You don't have to hide from me. Joey? Are you pulling a fast one?"

I'd set my camera down somewhere, but I still had my phone in my pocket. With shaking fingers, I tapped on the ReCord app. It was an old app that had come in handy back in the day. I'd caught more than a dozen EVPs using the older versions, and it had always been reliable. EVPs or electronic voice phenomena, which is the technical term for capturing inaudible voices, had been the thing to convince me the other side was real. Some people swore by their thermal cameras or their K2 meters. Not me. Give me audio proof. One thing I knew for sure was there was an afterlife, and lots of the earthbound dead wanted to talk about it.

I tapped on the phone and turned up the volume. "You really don't have to be afraid of me. I am not going to hurt you. I am here to listen. Please, tell me what you want."

A door slammed but not on my floor. It was beneath me and sounded like the backdoor slamming shut. Rather than chase the phantom visitor through the house and out into the yard, I crossed the landing and leaned over to get a good look at the neglected backyard. I knew from the description of the land there was a creek back there some-where, but I couldn't see it. The woods grew thick and wild on the Ridaught Plantation. I had every intention of having the mess cleaned up when I could afford it, but that's not what drew my attention.

There was a woman in the backyard.

I could only see the back of her, and she was definitely wearing white. A white dress, white shoes, and a tidy white hat. Her hair was dark brown, and she wore it slicked back at the nape of her neck. If I had to guess, I'd say a nurse, and she wasn't alone.

I caught my breath as I watched her push what I thought at first was an empty wheelchair, then I saw the faint outline of a figure, an older person with short white hair. As the phantom nurse pushed the wheelchair down the broken stone pathway, she twisted her neck slightly and glared at me.

She glared at me like she saw me and I was the reason she was leaving the house.

I had a strange thought. If this ghost was fleeing the house, fleeing the Ridaught Plantation, there must be a reason, and that reason wasn't me. I was no threat, and neither was Chloe. The apparition fluttered into nothingness before I could even formulate a sentence. I tapped on the phone screen and turned off the recording. I peeked outside again and saw it was starting to rain. The sky had turned slate gray, so this rain would be here a while. Lightning popped in the distance. Whoever she was, she had vanished. Seeing an apparition on the same day I heard screaming was like having back to back home runs, but I didn't feel afraid, or terrified. I felt kind of peaceful and thoughtful. I wondered what it all meant.

It was time to deal with the silverware and maybe make some coffee. I turned away from the window and was about to slide my phone back in my pocket when I noticed the blip on the screen.

The ReCord app had grabbed two items, two mini audio clips. One had to be me. I'd spoken once up here. I tapped on the screen to play them both. The first one was me, like I thought, only I sounded a little too loud and distorted.

Note to self, don't turn the app all the way up when using it. Apparently, they'd fixed the volume bug.

The second voice wasn't mine.

To quote my grandmother, "That ain't friendly."

There were only three words in the second clip, but I didn't need any software to decipher the meaning. This wasn't an archaic language like you'd see in a horror movie. They were pretty plain to me.

"GET OUT NOW!"

6

CHLOE

"You drive like a nun, Otis. Would you please get a move on? What year is this car anyway?" I teased my friend as his vehicle lurched forward. I wasn't sure he had this whole stick shift thing down, but as I wasn't riding the bus, I reminded myself not to gripe too much. It wasn't like I had a car.

Creepy Addams Family home? Check.

Nosy ghost with no consideration for personal space? Check.

Weirdo lady who thinks she's my aunt? Check.

Car? Nope.

"I should never have told you my middle name. No one calls me that except my grandmother, so unless you want me to start calling you Granny..."

I put my hands up as if to say, "I surrender." He grinned at me, showing me his perfect white teeth. His dang smile was impossible to ignore, and I really liked it, almost enough to kind of trust him. He wasn't really my type, if I could say I had one. The truth was I'd never even been on a date before, although I'd hung out with boys on many occasions, usually at the mall or at the gaming store, but always in a group setting.

I couldn't believe it when Tamara handed me gas money this morning. I had expected an argument, and I'd come downstairs mentally prepared to stand my ground, but the ghost demanded all her attention as usual. He was trying to kill himself, I guessed. Typical of him. Ever since we moved into the "old homestead," he'd made himself the center of attention, her attention at least. The upside was she wasn't constantly asking me if I was okay anymore, but I did feel lonely. Sometimes the ghost was too much. I'd already made up my mind I wasn't going to give him the time of day or acknowledge him ever again if I didn't have to unless he continued to plunder through my things. Then I'd have to figure out how to get rid of his skinny ghostly behind. The salt and sage weren't working as well as I'd hoped. Maybe if I did banish him, Tamara and I could have a conversation without his Caspar-y ass inserting himself.

Great. I was jealous of a ghost.

In the beginning, I thought I'd imagined Joey, at least the first time. I spotted him when I'd gone to the bathroom in the middle of the night. He'd been walking down the hall with a doo-rag on his head, only it wasn't actually a doo-rag. It was my favorite scarf, the one with the pixelated Pac Lady all over it. I went off on him without thinking that he wasn't a real guy, a real living guy. He'd tossed the scarf to the ground and vanished into the wall with a dramatic flair. I should have known then he'd be a problem.

But I hadn't dreamed him up. Joey was as real as Trey

Otis Armstrong. Tamara saw him too. The real twenty-thousand-dollar question was if we weren't both hallucinating, then where was my mom? Was it like it had been in life, she couldn't be bothered with her unwanted kid?

Didn't she love me enough to haunt me?

Nope. Instead, I was stuck with Joey.

The Splash Girls sang loudly from the car's scratchy speakers. I couldn't decipher what they were saying. They screamed too much for my liking, and I didn't care enough about the all-girl band to find the lyrics. Apparently, Trey liked them because he turned them up and kind of sang along.

Minus five points for his music choices.

I couldn't understand why Trey wasn't considered one of the cool kids. More than a few of the snobaritas, my verbiage for snobby girls who liked clustering up and being all cliquish, checked Trey out on the daily. In the beginning, a few of the more daring snobaritas tried to chum me up, but only to get the info on Trey.

They gave up pretty quick when I gave them the cold shoulder, but I'd made a few friends. None on the bus, though. Trey and I had hit it off almost right away.

I couldn't figure him out. Like me, he seemed to enjoy his own company. Nobody picked on him. He was too tall to be bullied, and he sat where he wanted at lunch. He was like Sweden. He was everyone's friend but nobody's best friend. Despite his handsome, southern boy looks, Trey Armstrong didn't hang with the in-crowd. He could certainly pass for the All-American jock type. I wondered why he didn't play football or basketball or something. Maybe he did, and I didn't know.

This is why I liked him. He was a complex character and kind of mysterious.

"How do you know how nuns drive? Have you ever ridden in a car with a nun?" he asked as he wheeled into the school and managed to park his rickety car without hitting the one beside it. "That's it, isn't it? You went to Catholic school?"

"No, Sherlock. I didn't go to Catholic school, and I have no nun friends. Should I put 'riding with nuns' on my bucket list?" I joked as I reached for my bookbag and the door handle. We were going to be late if we didn't get a move on. I might be a lot of things, like a loner, a gamer, and usually the smartest girl in the room, but I hated being late.

He turned off the car and reached for his book. Just the one book. Trey never brought books home with him, and I knew he got good grades. Was he really so smart he didn't have to study? "Hey, hold on a second. I don't know anything about you, Chloe. Not really. Tell me something."

"What?" I tucked my hair behind my ears, forgetting I liked keeping them hidden. They were monster-sized and my least favorite feature, along with my eyebrows. "We're going to get written up, Trey. Can we play Ten Questions later?"

His smile vanished but only briefly. It quickly returned with its usual brilliance. "Fine. Be evasive, Chloe. I like a challenge. Let's go before we get drenched. Need a ride home?"

"Yeah, and I've got some cash for you. Tamara says no freebies."

"What? That's ridiculous. I live right down the street. Shoot! It's about to pour. Let's go!"

We both took off running as the clouds burst above us. Suddenly, Trey's hand was in mine, and he was tugging me along to the covered sidewalk as if I couldn't figure out how to get there on my own. His skin was warm but not sweaty, and his touch was gentle but steady. It was the first time a boy ever held my hand and I loved every second of it. To my surprise, we weren't late. A few people gave us weird looks, and I quickly pulled my hand away. I hadn't been at this school long enough to commit to one boy.

Trey didn't seem to notice. He waved goodbye and headed toward his classroom as the first bell rang. In a matter of seconds, the hallway cleared, and the sky went so dark I turned to look behind me. The sudden storm had blown up fast and the doors, heavy as they were, hadn't shut all the way. Suddenly, they swung open, and a vicious wind blew down the hallway. I couldn't think why, but it felt personal—like the wind was coming for me.

"Don't worry about it, Miss Ridaught. I'll get it. Go on to class. You wouldn't want to get blown out the doors." Henry the janitor pushed his plastic garbage can to the side, and remarkably it didn't budge as he tucked his head down and walked to the door. I didn't correct him. He wasn't the first person to assume my last name was Ridaught. I did live at the Ridaught Plantation, but that wasn't my name. It had been my mom's before she got married, albeit briefly. My last name was Carol. Chloe Carol. What a joke of a name. Mom liked calling me CiCi, but I hated that. It was a stupid nickname for a kid unless you wanted that kid to become a stripper one day.

No thanks, Mom. One stripper in the family is enough. That will never be me.

I walked into the classroom, unaware that my skirt had blown up and my hair looked like I'd stepped out of a wind tunnel. "Hey, hold on a second." A girl next to the door, Nicole, reached for my skirt and rescued me from exposing my underpants to the entire school.

"Thanks," I whispered as I took my seat behind her and avoided making eye contact with anyone else. Our teacher, a boring man with a big mustache, went over the highlights of the chapter, but this was Monday, which meant reading day.

Sometimes, Mr. Owens had us read aloud, and on other days we "enjoyed" silent reading. I knew he had migraines, although I wasn't sure how I knew that. They were pretty bad too. He really needed to go see a doctor, but it wasn't my place to tell him. I was just another pimple-faced teenager in his classroom, with too much attitude and not enough brains.

If he'd hoped for silence today, he was out of luck. The big picture windows were distracting for the students. We weren't getting any reading done. The lightning and wind were impossible to ignore. Paper and debris blew around the concourse, and our classroom overlooked the edge of it. The school was built in a U-shape, and while not very large, it had been large enough to get lost the first few times here.

To my complete shock, I saw a man walking across the concourse. He didn't seem concerned about the dangerous lightning and the pelting rain, or that at any moment we might have a tornado barreling down on us. This felt like tornado weather. Didn't anyone else see him? As I thought that and watched the man cross the yard, I heard the loud-speaker announcement.

"Faculty and students, please shelter in the hallway. All classes, please proceed to the hallway."

The man kept walking. Where was he going? The class was practically running out to find shelter in the hallway, which seemed stupid. Who thought hiding beneath row upon row of metal lockers was a smart idea? Only me and Mr. Owens seemed to notice the man.

It wasn't a man, it was Joey. His tell-tale walk would give him away anywhere. He tended to swing his hands if he was stressed about something.

"Joey?" I whispered as I watched him come closer. The wind didn't wet his perfect hair, or even move it. He wasn't wet, but he was clearly vexed. Before I could say another word, Mr. Owens closed the blinds.

"You heard the principal, Chloe. In the hallway, please."

"But…"

He wasn't taking no for an answer, and I couldn't see Joey anymore. I wondered what was going on. Was it something at the house or Tamara?

Embarrassed and quite sure Mr. Owens had seen Joey too, I joined my class and took a spot on the floor. The lights flickered until finally, they went off completely. Someone was softly crying. The school shook like an angry giant had a hold of it and wasn't letting it go until it broke it into a hundred pieces. The creaking and moaning were unreal like something out of a horror movie. Who was crying?

I realized that someone was me.

An arm went around my shoulder. Trey was beside me, and his damp sweatshirt rubbed against my skin. The tornado roared over the school while the gathered students collectively screamed, and some prayed. Some were crying, like me. I wasn't afraid, not for myself, but I couldn't say what I was feeling.

Trey held me and whispered, "It's all right. We're going to be fine. Breathe, Chloe." I clung to his arm after the windows blew out in the classroom behind us. The crashing sound seemed to go on forever, and then it suddenly quit.

Everything got quiet. Far too quiet.

The air went eerily still, and the darkness vanished. The sky was kind of red-pink. "Oh, no," I heard the girl behind me say. It was the calm before the second half of this storm.

Joey was there too, on the other side of me. His arm encircled mine, and he kept his head down. What a weird sensation. Living warmth on one arm, and a cold, aching sensation on the other. I knew he couldn't help that he was dead, but Joey's afterlife state wasn't good for the living.

What are you doing here? I demanded. I wasn't speaking with my mouth, but with my mind. I knew for a fact it wasn't something Tamara could do, but we weren't related. Maybe this sort of mind-melding with a ghost only happened with people in my family.

Of course, Joey could hear me. We'd had more than a few arguments like this.

You should be with Tamara. Is she okay?

Fine, she's fine. Except for the others.

Trey started yelling, "Get down!" The roof of the

school lifted, but only a few feet. It was like that angry giant had started to pull it up but changed his mind. He didn't really want to tear up the school. Just the roof. It plopped down, and a few pieces of something fell to the ground. Then the roaring stopped. The tornado's strength had abated. I wiped away tears and kept my head down.

It's okay, Chloe. I'm here for you. I'm here to protect you because she can't come.

I peeked at him and couldn't stop myself from frowning. Why was I always frowning at the ghost?

You should have stayed with her, Joey. As you can see, I am fine. And why are you wearing my plaid shirt? What did I tell you about getting into my clothes? Wait a second, what do you mean, "she can't come." What's happened to Tamara?

My heart sunk until I heard his response.

Tamara is at home playing with the silverware. I'm here because your mom asked me to come. Nice lady. Too much lipstick, though. I thought this was Tamara's shirt. I found it in her closet.

The alarms were going off and the rain continued to fall, but there was no greater storm than the one in my heart. Joey faded like a shaken Etch-a-Sketch. He slowly evaporated and blended into the scenery. Nobody saw him. No one but me.

Thank you.

Joey did not answer. He was gone. Everyone was crying now, crying and swearing. Even the teachers. "Take me home, Trey. I have to go home."

Joey was gone, and I had to go too. I felt like I was going to have a panic attack if I didn't see Tamara. I had to make sure she was okay, and maybe, just maybe, I'd see my mom. If there was a chance, I had to try.

"After the storm is over, I'll take you home. We can't go out there now. Look, Chloe. People are hurt. Mr. Owens. Oh, God. I think he's bleeding!"

Our teacher was lying on the floor, a pool of blood beneath his head, but he was alive.

"Someone call 911!" Trey yelled.

7

ANNIE HENSLEY

1987

Marjorie's whimpers ended, but they were replaced with my own. It was odd to make such a sound. I didn't like hearing it. How many times had I heard the death rattle— the sound a dying patient makes?

Could I be dying? What was happening to me? The pain! Oh, the pain!

I desperately wanted to beg for my life, to plead with my shadowy attacker, but no sound would form in my throat. My attacker's grip was so tight around my throat I could feel the tiny bones in my neck weaken beneath his grip. With his hands still wrapped tightly, the shadow forced me against the wall, and we were face-to-face.

This was no shadow, no creature or ghost.

I knew this face.

I had worked with Paul West for months, but we hadn't said more than casual greetings. He worked the night shift while I worked days, and the only time we exchanged much more than a passing hello or goodbye was in concern for Marjorie. On more than one occasion, I had noticed some of her medication missing. I'd asked him about it and made a report, which was standard procedure. I couldn't fathom a reason for this terrifying assault.

Even though my mind raced and my heart beat heavily, my mind could not come up with a good reason for this violence.

Paul? I tried to vocalize his name to beg for mercy.

Marjorie! What had he done with her?

I had to survive, I thought even as my skin tingled from lack of oxygen. I knew enough about the dying process to know how things unraveled. For a second as he leaned in, I thought maybe he would let me go or assault me and be done with it, but he breathed on my neck and began speaking atrocious inappropriate threats, things that made me sick to hear them.

Suddenly, my summer self-protection training class at the YMCA came back to mind. As my ex-roommate used to say, "Dating in the 80s was a dangerous prospect." This wasn't a date. I brought my knee up as far as I could and contacted his gonads. Paul West immediately dropped to the ground with a growl of a threat in his mouth.

I fell back against the wall as he released me. I could hardly stand upright, but I was mobile enough to try and get away, and I had enough awareness to know I needed to do it quickly. I had to leave the Ridaught Plantation and find safety.

It was dark outside as I stumbled my way to the open front door. One hand rubbed at my throat while I felt my pockets for my keys, but they were gone. I must've dropped them during the assault, and I couldn't go back in there.

I didn't know how long it would take him to recover, and when he did, I would be in a worse situation. My white leather shoes tapped on the dirty floor as I ran. Paul cursed me from the other room. He was swearing at me and calling me profane names, which did not inspire me to linger.

"When I get my hands on you..."

I stumbled out the front door, scratching my knees and making one bleed, but the urgency of my situation wasn't lost on me. I ran down the driveway and raced toward my car. The doors weren't locked. What was I going to do now, hide in the car and lock the doors?

He could break the glass, and then what? I saw his grungy motorcycle. I had no idea how to drive one.

No! Run, Annie! Run for your life, girl!

I hurried toward the woods and whimpered as I stumbled through low patches of berry laden stickers. I glanced over my shoulder, but I didn't see him. Then I did, coming for me.

I screamed, but my voice did not cooperate. He'd damaged my vocal cords. I cried silently as I struggled to scream. I ran as fast as I could, but my legs were freezing, and my shoes were making an odd slapping sound as I flew deep into the woods. I ran toward a clearing in the woods in the hope of getting my bearings. Stars burned brightly above me, but I was no Girl Scout. I couldn't read the stars, but I knew the North Star. If I traveled in one direction, I was bound to make it to a road.

"Come out, come out wherever you are," Paul sang as if

we were two kids playing Hide and Seek. I took off again and moaned as a thin tree branch slapped me across the cheek. It stung, and I was sure it had drawn blood. Oh, God, please don't let me die out here, I thought.

I kept moving and in a few minutes, I heard the sound of running water. I'd gone in the wrong direction, away from the Crystal Springs Senior Home. I could still make it to the road if I kept going, but I'd have to swim across the creek and climb a steep embankment.

I was only a few feet from the creek when I heard a thunk and felt warmth on the side and back of my head.

Everything went black.

Forever.

8

TAMARA

I heard the tornado siren go off before I received a text message from the school district informing me the school would be closing due to inclement weather. I wasn't going to wait for the bus to bring Chloe home. I would haul ass to that school and get her myself. The sky had darkened dramatically, but I didn't have a clue bad weather threatened our area. I rarely paid attention to my weather app, and at some point, I must have turned off the notifications. I'd never been one to watch the news, not even local, but after the text, I decided I had to start paying attention to these things.

Despite the low hum of sirens, the tornado hadn't hit the Ridaught Plantation, but the school hadn't been that lucky. There was quite a bit of damage to Crystal Springs High School, according to the kitchen radio. Before I could get to the car, Chloe stomped through the back door, looking as if she'd run all the way home.

"Chloe, are you okay? Where's Trey? The school just

texted me about the tornado. I can't believe it. Are you hurt?"

The teenager's eyes were brimming with tears, but she didn't shed a single one. She didn't seem to want to talk either. I tossed my keys and purse on the counter and opened my arms to her, but Chloe snorted at the idea of hugging and eased around me instead.

That hurt, but this wasn't about me.

My natural inclination was to hold and comfort my late bestie's daughter, but she rejected any such idea. Despite her terrifying experience with a destructive tornado, she was her typical teenage Chloe Carol self. She stomped her thick-soled shoes as she burned through the kitchen like her skirt was on fire. Unfortunately, she noticed the stack of silver items I had not yet put away. She cocked her head at me as her natural frown deepened.

"What are you doing in here? Is this some sort of kooky ritual? I don't know how much more I can take, Tamara!"

I put my hands up as if I were fending off a physical blow. "Ritual? I don't do rituals, Chloe. I was actually going to ask you about this. Why don't you just take a deep breath and sit down? Need a glass of water?"

"I don't need water, Tamara. What is this?"

"It's a...I don't know what it is. I found it after you left."

She paused for a moment and asked, "Have you checked with the ghost? This looks like something he could pull off. Is that silver?"

"Joey didn't do this. Why would he? Are you really okay? Is Trey okay? I heard on the news that someone got hurt. You're acting really weird. Who got hurt?"

Chloe blinked at my questions and snatched her

sagging backpack firmly back on her shoulder. "Mr. Owens, but everyone else is fine. I'm going to my room."

"Not until we talk, Chloe. I'm worried about you." She left me standing in the kitchen with the creepy silver sculpture and murmured something like, "I don't have time for this."

"Time for what? Chloe? Don't you walk away from me." I followed her into the hallway as she completely ignored me and flounced up the wooden staircase.

I knew it had been a bad idea to encourage her to pick a bedroom on the second floor.

After all that happened today, the phantom screams, the poltergeist-like activity, and the tornado I felt really insecure about letting her go back upstairs. I needed to warn her, but first things first. "Come on, Chloe. Give me a break. I'm not the enemy. Please! Hold on a second!" My answer was a slamming door, which I proceeded to tap lightly on. "Please let me in. You shouldn't shut me out. Come on, Chloe."

"Go away," the teenager replied as she turned on her radio and turned up the volume. I thought I heard her crying, but it was hard to hear over the stylized vocalizations of her favorite pop singer. My hand reached for the doorknob, but I thought better of it.

It was never a good idea to force yourself into a teenager's presence. All that would happen was she'd resent me even more than she already did.

I could get any information I needed from the school. I paused one last time in front of her door and told her, "I'll be in the kitchen if you want to talk." All of my worries from the day dissipated in the presence of this current conundrum.

How in the world was I going to parent this child?

Maybe that was the problem. I was trying to be her parent, and she was never going to accept me as such. This wasn't good. If I couldn't comfort Chloe, the least I could do was figure out what was going on in the house. Something was happening here at the Ridaught Plantation.

As I went back downstairs, I whispered Joey's name a few times, but I got no response. Not a dang thing. He didn't pop out of a wall or step in front of me with a big smile on his silly face. It was so strange he wasn't all up in this mess. Usually, we were together constantly except for my time in the bathroom, which I had firmly forbidden him from entering. Not that he ever listened to me.

Nobody in this house listened to me.

What a weird day this had been. To establish a little normalcy, I encouraged myself to act like the grown-up I needed to be for Chloe and me.

I went to the kitchen and began disassembling the horrible structure on my kitchen table. Naturally, the silver clattered everywhere and made lots of noise, but finally, I got it taken apart and put back where it belonged, except for the silver cup, which I'd never seen before. I still didn't know where it had come from.

"Joey, this would be a great time to show up. I need some help here." Not a word. I grabbed my phone and took a few more pictures, focusing on the bottom of the cup. There was a strange marking, and it didn't look modern. I was no antique collector, but when I got a chance, I'd check it out. What an odd mark. It was a tiny, twisting fork icon. There were no numbers on the cup and no other marks except lots of tarnish.

I thought maybe if I cleaned it up, I'd find more clues.

I searched for the silver cleaner and got to work. A half-hour later, I was looking at a shiny silver cup, but there was nothing else to discover. It was clearly an antique. I took a few more pictures and then whipped up scrambled eggs while I watched the dark clouds diminishing from the bare kitchen window. I'd been checking my phone since Chloe came home, just in case this sudden storm cell erupted again. It fizzled out a bit before moving east. My scrambled eggs were tasteless, and I suddenly felt tired.

"Joey, where are you? You need to stop playing around. Joke's over. You got me."

After cleaning up my lunch, I paced the kitchen, expecting him to reappear with his head in the oven, but nothing happened.

There was nothing to see or hear except for the sound of Chloe's exceptionally loud radio from the floor above me. She had the world's most annoying song on repeat, and I had listened to it at least five times.

No Joey. No Chloe.

I was supposed to write a few chapters in my book. So far, I hadn't stuck with that plan, so I headed to the office to try to get a few words in. The day wasn't over yet. I'd sketched the outline of my ghostly tale a few weeks before, but filling in the blanks had proven to be challenging. Probably because I didn't know where the story was going.

Very much like my life.

They say life imitates art. Maybe it was the other way

around? I sat down to write something brilliant, but I got nowhere fast. In between writing a few dry sentences, I checked my email, but there weren't any responses to my current questions about the silver sculpture. The realty company sent me a few more listings, and I emailed them back, agreeing to show the houses later in the week. I needed a Plan A and a Plan B.

Possibly also a Plan C.

Focus, Tamara. I tapped the keyboard to breathe life into my main character, but I wasn't having much luck. This book wasn't happening today. I had too much on my mind, worry for both Chloe and Joey, to focus on my imaginary world. I found it ironic my character, a young woman named Jennifer, was also trying to solve a paranormal mystery. Jen's situation paled in comparison to what I faced, though. With a sigh of disappointment, I wandered around the house, sipping my lukewarm coffee. I kept to the bottom floor looking for clues, hoping to see something to explain all this.

The rain had stopped, and the dark clouds had blown away. There were no more threats of storms or tornadoes or anything deadly. I decided I needed to get out of the house for a while. I would lose it if I stayed there another minute.

I sent Chloe a text inviting her to tag along since banging on her door wouldn't get me anywhere. The music was so loud I doubted she'd hear me if I banged on it with a hammer.

Going to town. Might stop by the library. Want to come?

No.

We could grab some coffee or a burger?

No.

My thumbs hovered over the phone's keyboard, and I resisted the urge to type in a string of sentences I knew I would regret. Instead, I sent a smiley face and an okay, just like every other parent or guardian of a teenage girl.

This was my life.

I grabbed my purse and keys and walked to the back door.

"Joey? I'm going out for a while. Keep an eye on her, please. Be back soon."

Nobody answered.

Great. Even the ghost didn't care. Retrieving my keys and purse from the counter, I gave the kitchen door a good slam as I left the house.

9

KEVIN

Crystal Springs wasn't a very large town, but the library was huge, much larger than I expected. To be fair, the Crystal Springs library had inherited a lot of reference books from the neighboring library that had closed its doors about a decade before.

I learned this from the librarian who lurked over me as I filled out my library card. Imagine having to fill out another library card and being charged for it. I coughed up the $2, and after a few minutes, the librarian returned with a warm, freshly laminated card. I kept losing the damn things. I thanked her and headed toward the reference section. It was quiet today, except for a noisy water fountain. I'd always liked the place. It had a homey, mysterious ambiance about it, and at the end of every bookcase was a Narnia style lamp complete with a flickering light. The signage was quaint, and the place was full of dusty old books.

Since it was an old fashioned library without a computerized book catalog, locating some of the books I needed proved to be a difficult task at times. I could handle the Dewey Decimal System just as well as the next person, and I was pretty good at locating things on microfilm. I had an eye for scanning, or so I was told by my English teacher who remarked on my ability to comprehend large swaths of text in one sitting. I always suspected I had somewhat of a photographic memory. In a limited way.

I glanced down at the piece of paper I had brought with me and opened my notebook. If I was going to get answers about who Annie Hensley was, this was a good place to start. Her file lacked photographs, and there were no cuttings from the newspapers. There had been nothing except her vital information in the file.

Five-foot eight inches tall. One hundred thirty pounds. Relatively good health. Born on March 26th. Enjoyed traveling. She had no living relatives except for a sister who couldn't be located right away. She was later found serving time upstate for larceny. There was nothing to implicate Annie Hensley, and she'd had no criminal record, not even a traffic ticket. There was nothing unusual about the nursing assistant. Except that she was killed by a gunshot wound to the back of her head. The damage was horrendous. The whole side of her face had been blown away.

I checked again, but there had been nothing else in the files at the station. I had to do some legwork, and in order to do that, I had to review the newspaper articles. I put in a few phone calls to the law enforcement agencies in her hometown and expected to see some emails when I got back, but sitting around and waiting wasn't my style. I pulled up microfilms from the day Miss Hensley was found and backtracked from there.

Ten minutes into my research, I found what I was looking for, or at least a start. The body of Annie Hensley had been found on the Ridaught Plantation property, not too far from the house, and very near the creek. I drew back from my scanning session and blinked. I was getting a little headache, probably from too much coffee and not enough rest. I cracked my neck and reminded myself of what the stakes were. Sheriff Jarvis depended on me to solve this case. I was deep into the next few newspapers when I heard a familiar voice behind me.

Tamara Garvey.

I'd know that husky voice anywhere. I couldn't say why. I'd only met her a few times, but truthfully, I was still ticked off by that welfare check call earlier. I guess she thought small-town cops were stupid, and it might be fun to toy with them. She wasn't alone in that kind of thinking, but pranks weren't good for the community, and they weakened the local police force. What would happen if a serious call came in while I was answering fake scream calls? I shook my head at the memory and continued scanning the microfilm until I found another article about Annie Hensley.

In this article, they had the victim listed as thirty-five years old when in actuality, she was thirty-seven. I flipped through my notes to confirm it. Those kinds of errors were common in local newspaper articles. The Crystal Springs *Journal* had never been the most reliable rag. The *Register* usually got such details correct. Strange how they shut down and the half-assed *Journal* kept on printing.

Annie was a single woman with no children, and she had been a registered nurse, make that a nursing assistant, no surprises there. There was something I had not expected. Although Miss Hensley was found on the property, she didn't work there. The Ridaught Plantation had been empty for nearly twenty-five years before she'd been killed. There was the possibility squatters or unauthorized tenants killed her, but there was nothing to suggest that as a likely scenario. The adjoining property had been a senior citizen's home and was where Annie worked when she was killed.

I turned off the machine and jotted down notes in my book. I needed to find a map of the creek or at least a map of that area, then I'd go out and see for myself what I could find on the property. Probably nothing after all this time, but it was worth a shot. At least I'd get the lay of the land in my head. Small details sometimes mattered. I had a ton of questions. The coroner's report left out too many details. There was no mention of the caliber gun or any kind of gunshot stippling. The investigation file was just as bad as the newspaper reporting. There wasn't a single person of interest, not even a name on file, which was even stranger. It's like the community collectively shrugged when this woman was murdered and did not care that her body had been unceremoniously dumped by Black Snake Creek. Was nobody going to be held accountable for this woman's murder?

"Sorry, Annie," I mumbled to myself as I collected my things and headed to the map section.

"Oh, hi, Deputy Patrick."

"Miss Gentry," I said cautiously.

"It's Garvey." She frowned at me.

"Right. That's G-A-R-V-E-Y, right?" I asked as I instinctively reached for my notebook to write it down. I knew I hadn't been spelling her name Gravey or Gravy. Damn it if she didn't have perfect lips.

She crossed her arms and stared at me like I was stupid. "I'd think you would have my name, address, and social security number memorized by now. Yes. G-A-R-V-E-Y. Middle initial A. T-A-M-A-R-A. Not Tammy or any other variation of my name. What are you doing here, Deputy? Following me around?"

I made a whistling sound at that idea. "I'm pretty sure I got here first. I'm doing the same thing you are, Miss Garvey—looking up stuff. Sometimes we cops get out of the office. I'm here to do some research on a cold case."

Why did I tell her that? Why were my palms sweating?

"Me too. I'm writing a book."

The librarian eyeballed us but didn't say a word. She would if we pressed her. "I didn't know that. A writer, huh? What kind of writer?"

"Fiction. Suspenseful-type books. I'm sure it isn't as interesting as what you do."

"I don't know. I hate reading true crime since I seem to live it every day. Maybe I should read your books. Have you written anything I might have seen?" I glanced at the shelves knowing full well there wasn't any fiction back here. I liked making her feel uncomfortable for some warped reason. Her dark lashes fluttered as she avoided my stare. She glanced away and shook her head.

"Not yet, but soon. I better not keep you, Deputy. I'm sure you're on some life-saving mission here at the library." Was she being a smart ass? I decided to ignore the offhand comment.

"I presume writers need to possess quite an imagination to write fiction. Don't tell me you write ghost stories. Or murder mysteries. That would explain so much, Miss Garvey. Why else would you want to live in the Ridaught Dead House?" I asked with a half-laugh. I'd honestly never heard it called that. Not since high school anyway.

Tamara's hazel eyes flashed green. "Are you joking with me, Deputy? I told you before I didn't have anything to do with that scream. I'm not lying about that. I have no reason whatsoever to fictionalize what is happening in my own house."

The librarian interrupted our escalating conversation with a loud "Shh."

I didn't look in her direction, but neither did I move out of Tamara's way. She shifted in her boots and changed the subject politely. "Any word on the storm damage at the school? How is Mr. Owens? I would think you would be working on that. Not trying to pin a prank on me."

Oh, so you admit it was a prank. The words were on the tip of my tongue, but the librarian cleared her throat, and I finally tossed her a go away look.

"Yeah, that was a freak storm, wasn't it? Pretty extensive damage to the roof, but the school district is on it. Mr. Owens got whacked on the head but is expected to make a full recovery. I guess I better get back to the office. I hear we're having apple fritters today. Looking forward to your party, Miss Garvey. Maybe I'll stop by for a few minutes."

She didn't appear happy about that. "You don't plan on showing up in your uniform, do you? That would be a real downer, Deputy. People tend to enjoy parties better when they can let their hair down without worrying they'll be arrested."

I couldn't help but grin at her level of discomfort. My late mother's favorite saying came to mind. God don't like ugly, Kevin. "I haven't made up my mind yet. I better get back to work. Nice to see you." I didn't budge. I needed to get myself in gear, but I stood there grinning like a possum eating fire ants.

"Nice seeing you too. Have a nice day." Tamara tossed her ponytail over her shoulder. She didn't move either. Why was I so rude to this woman? It's not like she robbed the community bank or something. Tamara Garvey was a pretty woman with delicate features and slender hands. In those pretty hands, she held a book on the subject of poltergeists. See? If you look long enough, Kevin, you'll always find clues about who people really are, and what they are really up to.

"Welcome to Crystal Springs, Miss Garvey. I do hope you have a nice day." I didn't wait for her to respond. I left the library, forgetting all about the map I'd intended to copy. I'd just Google it. I had to get refocused on the task at hand.

"Bye," she said as I waved my hand and left. I turned the car toward Black Snake Creek and tried to put those lips of hers out of my mind.

It took a few miles to achieve my goal.

10

TAMARA

I came home with some books I hoped would help me understand the reason for the screams and strange goings-on at the Ridaught Plantation. Ridaught Dead House, indeed. What a stupid name.

There was a new stack of dirty dishes in the sink. The sounds of obnoxious music coming from the floor above me let me know she'd cloistered herself back in. How could one teenager manage to dirty two pots, plates, and silverware in less than two hours? Did she have a dinner party while I was gone?

I wasn't going to go up there and gripe about it right now, but I was definitely going to say something eventually. I made myself a glass of tea and tidied up the kitchen and then began flipping through the first library book. There was quite a lot of theory on the subject of poltergeists but nothing solid. I was surprised to discover there were many cases like mine, where metals like silver and gold had been reported to be used and manipulated by spirits.

One theory suggested the energies from those metals were easier for spirits to manipulate, or they were supernatural conductors, but the purposes and reasons for those types of strangeness were as of yet unproven. The most logical explanation I read was the moving of metals was some sort of communication, one that was foreign to living people. I didn't get it. What could that silver monstrosity possibly mean?

Maybe it was just meant to scare the living.

A chill went through my body as I pondered the page. I couldn't be sure. I closed the book and set it aside and debated whether or not to go back upstairs to try and mend fences with Chloe. I called out for Joey a few times and reminded him that Ghost Hunters was coming on in a bit, but I didn't hear a thing. Not a peep. The Ridaught Plantation felt strangely quiet and empty. Rain pattered on the roof, and the skies were dark again. Come to think of it, it hadn't been raining at the library, but here it had not stopped. It was as if some sort of gloomy rain cloud had settled over the Ridaught Plantation or the Ridaught Dead House as the deputy put it. It wasn't just the weather-related cloud. The whole place felt different. It was old and drafty and not modern, but it never before felt unwelcoming, at least not before the disembodied scream manifested or the silver piled up on the table. No, it had never felt dark, but it felt that way tonight.

I did a few other tasks that needed to get done like laundry and rearranging a few items in the hall closet, but there wasn't much else to do, and I was feeling a bit lost without Joey's company and Chloe's angst, snorts, and wide-eyed expressions.

What was life without a good eye roll from your teenager?

I went into the living room, which I thought might have been a parlor before, and I turned on the television. I texted Chloe, but naturally, she didn't answer me. Joey didn't show up either. This sucked. I watched a few episodes of a paranormal show and then decided to shower and get ready for bed. What a bummer of a day. No writing on my book and no calls about any of the houses I had listed in the newspaper. More money down the drain. Just more ridiculous behavior from the deputy and no love at all from Chloe.

I clicked off the television and went to my bedroom. It was as messy as ever. I thought if I left clothes lying around, Joey might show up. He hated clothes on the floor and disliked even worse an untidy closet. I climbed into bed and laid there, staring at the ceiling.

"Joey, I wish you'd get your skinny ass back here. Whatever you're doing, I hope you're okay."

It wasn't Joey who opened the door to my room, but Chloe, looking like she had been crying all day. I sat up in bed. "Chloe? Are you okay?" She sobbed as she collapsed beside me, and I held her like she was my own. I couldn't make sense of what she was saying. Her face was smothered in the pillow, but I gathered it was about her mother, the tornado, and something about Mr. Owens. I didn't know what to say or do.

"I'm so sorry, Chloe. I saw Deputy Patrick at the library. He told me Mr. Owens was going to be all right. I'm sorry about everything."

Chloe continued to cry, and I handed her a wad of

tissues from the box on my nightstand. We didn't talk, not really. There wasn't much to say. I glimpsed the alarm clock and saw it was after midnight. Chloe snored lightly, and I resisted the urge to move the hair out of her face. I never in a million years would have imagined I would be a foster mom. Or was the term *ipso facto* mom? I couldn't say for sure. Sad fate had brought us together, and I felt grateful.

Chloe didn't look much like Tina Louise, but the dancer I knew had always sported bright red hair, a painted-on beauty mark, and ridiculously long eyelashes. Chloe had Tina Louise's upturned nose and sculpted brows, but that was where the similarities ended. I could be wrong. If anyone understood the power of makeup and a wardrobe made of sequins and feathers, it was me. No, Chloe wasn't like us, not like her mom, and definitely not like me. She was a natural beauty. She didn't need all the "extras," and if I had anything to do with it, she'd never have to strap on a pair of high heels and go to work.

I sighed at the thought and imagined Chloe walking across the stage as a high school graduate, and then a college graduate and walking down the aisle to get married. Having two-point-five children and living here at the Ridaught Plantation, which had become a successful bed and breakfast. I had so many dreams for this child and no idea how she felt about any of them.

I've got this, Tina Louise. Your little girl is safe with me. I swear I'll do my best to keep her on the straight and narrow, but she's kind of a pain in the ass, like her mother.

I didn't hear any response. I'd already tried doing some

EVPs when we first moved in. I'd heard nothing at all from my late friend. From what the lawyer told me, nobody had lived here in years. Not even Tina Louise. She'd inherited the place a few years before she died but never took up residence. It had been her mother's property and her mother before her and so on. It was meant to be Chloe's.

I was going to make sure that happened, darn it.

After a while, I fell asleep, although I couldn't seem to get into a deep sleep. The house popped, and floors creaked, and my eyes flew open with every sound. Thankfully, there were no phantom screams or anything else coming from the top two floors, and nothing else happened either.

I finally sank into a deep sleep and got an hour or two before my alarm squalled. Chloe was already up, and I could hear her walking around in her room, music playing softly. At least it wasn't the Sparkle Girls or whoever the hell those screaming banshees were the other day. Ugh, modern music.

The memory of Chloe's tears warmed my heart, and I sighed with mixed emotions. I hurt for Chloe, to miss her mother so badly, a mother she hardly saw when she was alive. Tina Louise's life had been centered around her career. Like many women in our profession, Tina Louise wanted to be discovered, to land that acting job, to be a celebrated centerfold, but she never quite made it. The sad thing was that right before she died, Tina had talked about making some changes. She wanted to spend more time with her daughter, and maybe go back to college.

It never happened.

I was glad she trusted me with Chloe but never understood why. I was just another dancer, a friend with similar struggles.

Chloe resented me, and would never say she needed me. Maybe she didn't, but I craved her needing me. I needed Chloe as much as she did me. Probably more, if I were honest.

Now, if only Joey would come back. Then he was there.

"Good morning, sunshine. My word, you look like Meow Kitty's leftovers." Joey leaned over me, his blond bangs carefully arranged in a gel-heavy Jersey Shore style. Did ghosts have access to hair gel? His strands were sticking straight up, but the sides were slicked back carefully. Oh, damn. He'd been in my hair products again. He was dressed in black, definitely not his normal attire, and was holding a raggedy-looking calico cat. Was it dead? It was moving, but it damn sure wasn't alive.

The cat meowed in agreement. As Joey leaned over me, I caught a glimpse of a gold chain around his neck. I'd never seen that before.

"Joey? Where have you been? What the hell is that thing, and what's up with your hair?"

The cat, clearly offended, hissed and bounded out of Joey's arms. It disappeared before it landed on the floor. For some reason, the strange movement made me yelp. Like having a ghost guy in my bedroom wasn't spooky enough; the cat put me on edge big time. Would it pop out somewhere and smack me when I least expected it?

"Great, Felicia. Do you know how long it took me to wrangle that cat? Your coffee is ready, Your Majesty, if you think you're getting out of bed today." He snapped his fingers at me and sashayed to the bedroom door.

"Of course, I'm getting up, but no cats, Joey. Especially no ghost cats. I'll meet you in the kitchen. Have you seen Chloe?"

"Where does it say I can't have a cat?" Joey asked as he posed in front of the door with his hand on the frame. "It's not like we have a rental agreement, Miss Realtor. Yes, I've seen Chloe. She's about to jet. By the way, you're the talk of the neighborhood, thanks to Linda Blabbermouth next door. She's talking up this party, and everyone in the county is coming. That sneaky B wants to have a séance in the attic. Want me to haunt her?"

I rubbed my face with both my hands and snorted at him. "What? Say that again? Only slower, please?"

"Ugh. You and your coffee addiction."

"I heard the word séance. There will be none of those. What are you doing hanging out at Linda's house? Is that where you've been? I was wondering where you popped off too, you big pain in the ass. Can't you stay close to home?"

"Girl, this was never my home. You don't know how crafty this Linda character is. She honestly thinks she's a psychic. I'd love to scare the hell out of her just once. Maybe poke my head out of her mirror while she's putting on that yard-sale lipstick. I mean, what color is that? Pig's Ass Pink? Ratchet."

"I think the word you're looking for is 'wretched."

"She's that too."

I laughed. "Joey?"

"Yeah?"

"I'm glad you're back."

He smiled and walked out of the room without any further explanation. I smiled, happy my ghostly companion had returned, even though he was his usual elusive self. I had no idea why he stuck his head in the oven the other day, and I would get to the bottom of that, but I was also going to ask about the nurse and the disturbing silver sculpture too. He was a ghost, he should know about ghostly things.

Grabbing my blue jeans and a rock 'n' roll t-shirt, I got dressed as quickly as possible. The floor was chilly beneath my feet, so I slid on a pair of unmatched socks, brushed my teeth, and pulled my hair into a ponytail.

Joey was back! It was sad that my healthiest relationship, or at least my happiest, was with a ghost.

To be fair, I was new to town and didn't know too many people. Except for Deputy Patrick. I wasn't sure why I was thinking about him. I pinched my cheeks to give them some color. No makeup today. It was time to do some detective work right here at home.

If Joey was right, my neighbor planned to turn my party into a paranormal fiasco. I wasn't going to allow Linda whatever her-last-name-was to steal this opportunity from me. I normally excelled at meeting people, and I wanted to establish us as desirable new residents of Crystal Springs. Not for my sake but for Chloe's. She was going to have to live here after I was gone. I still hadn't made up my mind where I was going to go, maybe California, but that was at least four to six years because college took years to finish. Maybe I would go back to college too.

It would be a hoot, the two of us in college together.

Chloe wouldn't go for that. She could barely stand being in the same house with me most of the time. I was still determined to put the Ridaught place back on the map. We were a bunch of kooks, just a weird family who called this place home. I needed to succeed as a realtor, too, because someone had to keep the lights on here, right? Chloe's inheritance was still in flux, and there was no way Joey could contribute to our bottom line.

I couldn't even imagine Joey having a job when he was alive. I knew so little about him. If he was going to be my friend, he was going to have to come clean about a few things.

"Where have you been? Were you hanging out next door?" I asked as I joined Joey in the kitchen. He was already sitting at the table with his usual Hello Kitty mug, just like mine. A kind of fog hovered over the phantom mug as if the coffee inside was smoking hot. It was kind of disturbing when I thought about it, and I shivered as I filled my mug.

Joey moaned his displeasure at my questioning. "Ugh. Stop nagging. You sound like my m…. Never mind. Is this what it's like to be married to you?"

I narrowed my eyes at him. "I don't know. I've never been married. How about you?"

"No interrogations before coffee, please. I swear, that cop is rubbing off on you."

I snorted in response as I dumped a few teaspoons of sugar in my coffee.

Unfortunately, the coffee wasn't that hot. Chloe must've made it hours ago. I popped it in the microwave and waited for it to heat up. With crossed arms and narrowed eyes, I continued my soft interrogation of him. "Why don't I know anything about you, Joey? Like your last name or where you're from or how you...well, you know. How you transitioned."

I was referring to how he died, but he artfully avoided the question by saying, "I never went that far. You can be gay and not transition. No offense, but I don't want your body."

"What?" I laughed, forgetting that I'd meant to demand answers from him. "I wasn't saying that. I am not against that. I mean, I stand in support of..."

"Oh, don't get in a tizzy, hon. I never wanted to be female. I have never had the desire to transition. It's okay for those that do, though. I am perfectly happy being my little old self. What do you think about today's look?" He cocked his head and pursed his glossy lips as he pointed to his overglazed hair. I removed the cup from the microwave and sat down across the table from him. If I got too close, I got cold. I was chilly enough this morning.

"Very Richie B, Joey. Looks great on you. Kind of nineties, though, huh?"

He leaned forward and sighed. "Hey, those wrinkles aren't looking any better. Maybe we should do some online shopping later. Pick up some wrinkle cream, and you're out of hair gel. They say that Hydroxy X is great for wrinkles and age spots. You've seen the commercials."

Sadly, I *had* seen the commercials. There were plenty of them between the late-night ghost hunting shows.

"Don't start that again. I don't have age spots, and you need to quit suggesting I have wrinkles. Please stop avoiding my questions, Joey. Where did you go? Who the hell was screaming in the house yesterday? Why was the silver stacked up on the table like some sort of Beetlejuice statue?" Joey's hand went to his chest as if to show me how shocked he was.

"*Beetlejuice*? Oh, God! I hate that movie! Did you have something like that here?"

"No, not Beetlejuice. But the silver. It was all here on this table, including that cup over there. Have you ever seen it before?"

"Silver cup? I don't know anything about a silver cup. Are you accusing me of stealing? I just used some hair gel, and I borrowed Chloe's scarf, but I'm bringing it back if I can remember where I put it. Gosh, y'all are so uptight."

"Nobody accused you of stealing. So you don't know anything about the silver piled up on the kitchen table? Is that what you want me to believe?"

Joey's perfect eyebrows arched high as he expressed his annoyance. "It might be some of those waywards y'all have walking around here. To be honest, I don't like visitors. There's only room for one ghost at this plantation, and that's me."

"'Waywards?' What are you talking about?"

"Honestly, I wasn't going to say anything, but as I am being accused of messing with the silver, I'll just go on and speak my mind. Clearly, you have mediumistic tendencies, Tamara."

"What?" I laughed at his suggestion.

"You wouldn't be seeing me if you didn't. To make matters worse, Chloe's aura is getting brighter every day. You two need to tamp it down a bit, or we'll have every stray in the county traipsing through the halls." He sipped his coffee and gave me one of his head tilts.

"Tamp what down? What are you talking about?" To think I missed him. He was so unhelpful I wanted to choke his ghostly neck.

"You two need to cut out all this mumbo-jumbo stuff. You writing that ghost story, which is quite frankly not great, and Chloe and her meditation. Between the two of you, we are going to be inundated with ghosts. There's a whole slew of ghosts in those woods, and they're like dogs that caught the scent of something. You are something. They know you're here, but so far, they haven't been able to find you. Not many of them anyway. It doesn't help that Linda Blabbermouth is playing with tools she's not qualified to use next door."

I couldn't believe my ears. "Nobody's doing anything like that. I'm just writing a book, and Chloe is just being Chloe. She does yoga, Joey, as you well know. Besides, you were here when we got here. What slew of ghosts are you talking about?"

He reached across the table and took my hand. His touch left it bone achingly cold. "You have no idea, do you? None at all. Oh, sweetie. You're just blind."

"Enlighten me," I said, trying not to feel desperate. I didn't want to move my hand, but it was freezing. "Who is the person screaming on the second floor, Joey? One of those ghosts from the woods?"

"Honey, you got me. I heard it, and I was like, gone."

"Yeah, but you came back and were standing next to Linda with those ridiculous curlers in your hair. You were mouthing something to me. What were you saying?"

He waved his ghostly hand absently. He suddenly appeared a bit faded, like he did when he was about to flicker out. "I can't remember. That was forever ago."

"No, it wasn't. It was only yesterday. You're telling me you don't know who was screaming on the top floor or how the silverware got stacked up on the table? What about the dead nurse? Surely you saw her outside. She was pushing a wheelchair."

He leaped to his feet. "Just because I am not of the living persuasion, it doesn't mean I know every dead person in the area. Give me a break. That's not how this works."

I could see how this was going. I was supposed to be a good friend and pretend he wasn't dead, just different. I couldn't mention his death, but he could stick his head in the oven and try to kill himself in front of me. Like most of my relationships, this was extremely frustrating. I opened my mouth and let it all fly.

"What the hell, Joey? I've got a Halloween party coming up and a teenager depending on me to keep her safe. Having dead nurses and random screamers hanging around isn't good for raising a kid. And she's all I got. I can't lose her, Joey. Do you understand that? It's not about the money. I will always make it. As long as I have brains, I'll make it. But I can't do this by myself."

He sat back down, his glossy lips expressing his sadness perfectly. I sometimes forgot how handsome Joey was when he wasn't wearing a doo rag or curlers. Even with gelled up hair, he was handsome.

"Oh, sugar. I'm so sorry. I had no idea you were under that kind of pressure."

"Well, I am. And another thing: there is another aunt, her

real aunt, who could at any moment say, 'Hey, I want Chloe.' Then she'd be gone, and she's all I got. You and her. How sad am I?" I sat at the table and fought the urge to cry like Chloe cried last night. Joey put his whole arm around me and tried to hug me without much success. I wanted to tell him he was giving me the creepy crawlies, but I didn't have the heart. He was trying to be a decent friend, bless him.

"Nobody is going to take Chloe away from us. We're family. I know you don't know me that well, but I love being here with you too. It's just the rest of those dead people who worry me." He got up and wandered to the kitchen window to look outside. Joey Whatever-His-Last-Name-Was had become a true friend. I didn't want him to leave. Not ever.

Joey's eyes widened as his mouth displayed a perfect O. "I know what we need to do! We need the Ghost Hunters to come! Call Quinton! He's so hot!"

I couldn't disagree fast enough. "No, I'm not calling anyone in, but you have given me an idea. We could have our own investigation. I have all the equipment: K2 meters, digital recorders, and even a thermal camera. Yes, we can do it all ourselves." My mind raced with the possibilities.

Joey twisted his lips thoughtfully. "Not Quinton?"

"No. I don't know Quinton, but I've got friends, or acquaintances, still in the field."

"Fine. We'll try it your way first. I'm in, but aren't you worried?"

"Worried?"

"About the ghosts in the woods. There's a lot of them. If

you start ghost hunting here, you might draw them in. Let me just say, if you think having a cat around is a problem, you're really going to have a problem with some of them. They look completely wretched. Talk about the living dead. Disgusting!" He visibly shivered, and with every shiver, he faded a little more. His concerns were legitimate.

"We'll do it strictly by the book, Joey. Pure science. No Ouija boards, and I'm sure as heck not sanctioning a séance. No way, no how. I hate to break it to you, but we've already got a ghost here besides you. If you weren't screaming and Chloe and I weren't, someone else is already here."

"Oh, God! Don't say that."

"They are already coming in, Joey."

He paced the kitchen. "Oh God oh God oh God!"

"Calm down. Enough of that. It's going to be okay. The sooner we figure out who's here, the sooner we can get rid of them. I better go upstairs and talk to Chloe. I think she'll be on board, but if not, it'll be you and me. Can I depend on you? I don't want to put you in a bad position. I mean, I don't want you to get bullied because you're helping the living."

He shuddered one last time. His faded appearance worried me. "This is our home. We can't let some screaming banshee roam the halls. But no hinky stuff. I'm serious. I already feel kind of pale. Talk to Chloe, please. Her meditation crap is making me sick."

"Okay." I had no idea what he was talking about. "How about 9 o'clock tonight? You rest up, and I'll get everything ready. I've got to dig all the equipment out unless you'd like to help me."

With a sad smile, he said, "Later." He vanished, taking all the warmth of the kitchen with him. It was weird. Usually, rooms got warmer when Joey departed them. I'd think about that later.

I headed upstairs and hoped for the best.

11

TAMARA

To my surprise, Chloe was down for ghost hunting with me. I didn't think it prudent to mention Joey was tagging along too. She'd figure it out soon enough. She didn't have much to say about what happened last night, and I didn't want to pry. It was enough to know she needed me, once in a while. I liked that. We had fallen into an easy peace with one another that I was loath to disturb, so I didn't ask her about whatever meditation activity was getting on Joey's nerves.

Joey showed up early and hung out in my bedroom while I got dressed in the closet. I didn't mind. He insisted I wear one of my old ghost-hunting shirts, so I picked a black one with red lettering. It had been a gift from a team that brought Tina Louise and me in to investigate a school with them. It was one of those pay-to-attend deals, but it had been a great experience. I would never have imagined a school to be a haunted place, but that one had proved to be downright creepy. It was a deserted elementary school. The acronym for this particular paranormal group was laughable. PADS: Paranormal Agents and Detective Society. To this day, I had to shake my head. I was so glad I wasn't a member of the group. Joey got a big old kick out of it. I thought it was stupid too, but at least it was a clean shirt.

Joey was wearing a Ghost Hunters t-shirt and black jeans with the same ridiculous-looking hairstyle. He'd been telling the truth. He'd gotten into my hair gel, but how he managed it I had no idea. He certainly wasn't going to tell me more than he wanted me to know. He showed me his shirt, and I gave him a thumbs up even though the back of the shirt was faded, like faded chalk, and his feet weren't visible. I hoped he would be okay and this investigation didn't affect him negatively. At least the mangy ghost cat wasn't around. I did spend a little time before our appointment this evening digging around in my plastic tubs for the necessary equipment. Naturally, all the batteries were dead, so I made a trip to the dollar store and replaced them all. Then it took a few minutes to show Chloe how to use each item. The three of us gathered in the hallway, and I piled the devices on the rickety hall table.

"Try the temperature gauge, Chloe. It's easy to use. Just move it up and down slowly."

Her response was an eye roll. "Please. Like I don't know how to use this thing. It's not rocket science, Tamara. It's a thermometer. We don't even know if these things work."

Joey walked into the hallway with us. "Of course, they work, girlfriend. She's just trying to show you how to work it."

"Great. He's going to hunt ghosts with us? Do I need to state the obvious here? Give me the dang thermometer. I guess it's as good as we're going to get since the ghost won't help us. Why can't he just tell us where the rest of them are and shoo them away?"

Joey swung around with his hand on his hip. Chloe stomped her foot as if it would frighten him away. The two were determined to have it out. "Again with the indirect questions, Chloe? His name isn't 'the ghost.' It's Joey, and he is standing right there. I know you can see and hear him. Why don't you ask him yourself because he's not telling me anything."

We both turned to our resident spirit, who was busy waving his hand over the antenna of a K2 meter and laughing about the lights coming on and off. "Oh, my God! This is fantastic. Look. You two try it."

Chloe barked at him, "You're not helping. You're going to wear the batteries out. Don't you know ghosts drain batteries? Do us a favor and don't touch anything."

He gave her the stink eye. "Don't touch anything? How am I supposed to help with this investigation if I can't touch anything?"

"Okay, you two. Just stay with me and watch yourselves. Enough of this chitter-chatter. Enough!"

"This whole investigation is going to be a nightmare," Joey declared in an angry yet much quieter voice. Joey didn't get angry about much, but he didn't like being mistreated or reminded he was dead. Chloe was going out of her way to aggravate him.

"Let's stick to the facts then, Joey. You do have a tendency to drain batteries. You can't help it, but that does mean no equipment for you. I know you don't want to give off a false positive. It's not you we're looking for. Chloe, dial back the antagonism or we'll be chasing our own tails tonight. You haven't heard the Screamer, but we have, and I wouldn't want to meet that thing in a dark alley. It was on your floor. I'd think you'd want us to find it."

"Who named it the Screamer? I don't like that."

"I did. Now shut up."

Nobody said a word, but they both glowered at me.

Perfect. They hated me. I could live with that. It sounded like a perfect parenting plan.

Chloe broke the silence. "Fine, we'll start upstairs. That's where you guys said you heard the scream." Chloe instructed in a very grown-up tone of voice. She left Joey and me in the hallway and headed toward the stairs. He stuck his tongue out at her back, and it was my turn to roll my eyes and sigh in an exasperated fashion.

"Sounds great to me, Chloe. Are you sure you're up for this? You can't take off screaming if you hear or see something."

"I'm ready, but do we really have to turn the lights off? Can we at least leave the hall light on?" When I was a newbie at investigation, I used to think the networks filmed these shows in the dark for better ratings. I mean, come on. It's creepy to see those green, ghostly images on the screen. As it turns out, spirits prefer moving around in the darkness. Except for my friend. Joey didn't like dark rooms.

"We're going lights out. That's the way I've always done it, and that's the way we're going to do it tonight. We're just looking for evidence, that's all. We're not coming to pick a fight. Just a few hours."

"Maybe he should go back to where he came from until

we're through, or else we aren't going to find a thing." Chloe flipped on the infrared camera as she turned out the lights on the staircase. At least she didn't call him The Ghost. Once all the lights downstairs were off, I grabbed the K2 meter and the digital recorder. I put my finger to my lips to remind Joey to be quiet. His footsteps sounded extremely heavy.

Joey lingered behind me and every few steps, he asked, "Did you hear that?" After the third time before reaching the top of the staircase, both Chloe and I turned and gave him the Look. "Yes, I hear you stomping up the stairs."

"What? I can't help it."

As we stepped onto the top landing, I watched the lights on the K2 meter bounce. All the lights were out except for one small lamp in Chloe's room. She hurried inside to turn it off and I held my breath. Joey was right. There was nothing but blackness up here. No stars shone, and there was no moon out. There was nothing to illuminate the upper hallway. I held my ground and evenly moved the K2 meter left to right repeatedly, but the device picked up nothing.

I felt Joey's cold hand on my shoulder. "Tell me that's you," I whispered to him.

"Of course, it's me. Who else would it be? What do we do first? You're the expert, right?"

"I think we start with an EVP session. Let's start here in the hallway and then down there, in that room. That's where I heard the voice."

"When did you hear a voice? You didn't tell me that, Tamara. Oh, my God! What did it say? Oh, I think I'm going to have a panic attack." Chloe stepped closer to him and shushed him. I ignored Joey's silliness and didn't take time to answer his questions. The more alarmed he became, the brighter he glowed. He looked like a drunken lightning bug at the moment, flickering on and off. Chloe was right. It was probably a bad idea allowing Joey to investigate with us, but how was I going to prevent it? I'd never investigated with a ghost before. His presence might have the opposite effect and attract a few ghosts. Or repel them. I couldn't be sure, but I had to work with the crew I had. The dead and the living.

"You two settle down." I clicked on the digital recorder. "I'm here to communicate with whoever is here," I said in a confident, loud voice. "I have a few questions I think you could help me with. Can you help me?"

"Really? You talk like you want it to help you with a test or something," Chloe criticized me with an edge of sarcasm as she held the camera up and fiddled with the buttons.

Joey faded in and out and whispered, "She's right, Tamara. This isn't how Quinton does it at all. Maybe we should call in a professional?"

I ignored their distrust. "My name is Tamara Garvey, and this is Chloe and Joey. What's your name?" I asked as I waited a few seconds and ignored their mutual snickering. So I choked up. Why I gave my last name, I'll never know. In a whisper, I instructed, "Chloe, keep an eye on that screen. Tell me if you see anything. Joey, try to stop glowing. It's distracting." With the digital recorder in one hand and the K2 meter in the other, I began to go deeper into the session. Joey still glowed slightly but not enough to affect anything. Chloe pointed the infrared camera at him, and he scowled at her.

"Stop it. That thing puts ten pounds on me."

"He looks crazy. Look at this. Wow, dude. You've got quite the aura. I've never seen this many colors on one screen before."

"I mean it. I don't want my picture taken!" Joey gave her the stink-eye and snapped his fingers above his head, disappearing like he'd performed a magic trick.

"Shoot. I ticked the ghost off. Sorry."

I side-eyed Chloe but kept going. "Is there anyone here? My friends and I are not here to hurt you, we just want to talk." I waited a few seconds, which felt like an eternity before asking another question. I forgot how long this process took. "What is your name? Can you say it really loud into this little light? If you do, I can play it back and hear it."

"Why are you here?" Chloe touched my arm as if to ask for permission, and I nodded at her. "Are you the screaming woman? Did you die up here? Were you murdered? Is that why you're screaming?"

Although I couldn't see him, I heard Joey gasp at the question, and before I knew it, his invisible fingers were gripping my shoulder tightly. It was so tight I had to brush his hand away. "Stop grabbing me, Joey." This was turning out to be a joke of an investigation. I played a little bit of the recording back at full volume, but there wasn't anything to hear, just the sound of my own voice and the two smart asses with me. I sighed and paced the room to give myself time to think.

"Please, you can't hide up here. Tell us your name, at least. Don't you have anything to say? Anything at all?"

"Wait a second," Chloe said slowly. "I'm picking up an

anomaly. There! At the end of the hall. Like it's poking its head out and then hiding again. That better not be you, Joey. See? In and out. In and out. Let's get closer." Fearless and determined, Chloe inched toward the room at the end of the hall. It was on the left side, exactly where'd I'd heard the voice whispering when I'd followed Deputy Patrick upstairs.

"Wait," I said as we got closer. I couldn't say why, but this felt wrong. All of it felt extremely wrong. The atmosphere was heavy, and it was getting hard to breathe. A strange itchy feeling crept over me. I remembered I'd experienced this sickening sensation before at Pennhurst. Man, I hated that place. The pitch blackness up here didn't dampen the escalating fear. My heart beat so loudly I was certain Chloe could hear it.

"I'm not going to run away. You need to talk to us. This is our house now. Our space. You need to tell us your name, please."

The answer was a bloodcurdling scream.

Only it wasn't the screamer I was looking for. It wasn't a female in agony or a child in pain like the scream I'd heard the other day, the one that had incited a cop coming to the house. That was very much the scream of a man.

A terrified man. Joey!

Suddenly he was back in full force and gripping my shoulder again. As I glanced behind me, trying not to pass out, I saw Joey glowing like a hundred-watt bulb.

"Are you trying to kill me?" I complained. That was when I saw what the screaming was about. Chloe was swearing under her breath and backing away as we both noticed a hooded figure at the end of the hall. It was blacker than black, and it was watching us. My hand immediately went for the light switch. I flipped it on because usually, light repelled a manifestation, but the dark figure remained.

Joey and Chloe screamed in unison and practically knocked me down as they fled. The black-clad monk figure stepped back and vanished into the wall.

I couldn't get out of the hall fast enough. As I scurried down the stairs behind the two terrified investigators, I began to rethink my life.

"Did you see that? Oh, my God! Did you see that?" Chloe was talking ninety miles to nothing while Joey blinked in and out and fanned himself like a crazy person. "It was there the whole time. What was it? The Grim Reaper? Do we have a reaper in the house? Why is it here, Tamara? Oh, my God! How am I ever going to sleep up there?"

I might need help, but who was I going to call? I could only think of one person. One local person, anyway. Boy, was he going to love hearing from me. How was I going to get Deputy Patrick to take me seriously and not put me away? Chloe was shaking. Her face was pale, her curls wildly framing her heart-shaped face. For the first time, I could see the resemblance between Chloe and her mother. *Dang it, Tina Louise! Why did you have to leave me your kid? I love you, but I don't want to do anything except get the hell out of here.*

"You two calm down. Stay here, Chloe. I'm going back upstairs. You keep Joey close. Joey, are you listening? You stay here and keep Chloe safe." I was talking all kinds of brave, but it was the last thing I was feeling. Time to get it together, Tamara Garvey. Woman up.

"You can't leave us. Are you sure you want to go back up there? Oh, my God. I can't believe I saw that…whatever it is. What is it?" She was close to tears, but I couldn't stop and comfort her. If I did, she'd be scared to death for the rest of her life, and I wouldn't have the courage I needed to get answers. Joey lingered close to Chloe as she plopped down on the padded bench in the downstairs hallway.

"I don't know, but it's not friendly. Joey, what do you think? Do you know who or what that is?" I asked, hopefully.

"Really? What, because I'm a spirit and he's a…whatever, I'm supposed to know him? Way to stereotype a person. Later." He flickered away, and Chloe frowned at the emptiness beside her.

"Typical. He's not good in a crisis. Or in everyday life. Now, what's your plan? The Ghost isn't going to babysit me, Tamara." She raised the camera as she stiffened her back. "If you're going back up there, I'm going too. You shouldn't do this by yourself."

"There's no need to—" I began, thinking I could talk her out of it.

"This is all real, isn't it? All of it."

I shook my head in disbelief. "Of course, it's real, Chloe. Joey is real. You've seen him every single day since we got here."

"I know you're fond of him, but do you think he has something to do with that horrible thing being here? I mean, if there's one, doesn't it attract others? He could be causing all of this. Why not get rid of him? Let's burn some sage, cleanse the house, and be done with it. Get rid of everything. Forever."

"Whoa, Chloe. That's the nuclear option. We've just started our investigation. I can't and won't do that to Joey, and I don't believe you really feel that way. Joey isn't evil. He doesn't deserve that. He's lost and confused. If I can help him, I will, and I can't do that if I push him out of here. Surely you see that. Wait a second. Is that what Joey was talking about? Have you been saging your room?"

"It's my room, isn't it? He won't stay out of my clothes."

"What else have you been doing? I need to know."

"I don't know. Meditation? That's all. I haven't been doing anything wacky like holding séances or playing with Ouija boards. I just don't want him in my room."

"I guess I can't tell you what to do in your own room, and Joey shouldn't be invading your space, but please don't hurt him. Give me time to help him move on."

"Is that really the goal? You want to help him move on?"

"Yes, that's the goal," I confessed. Even as I said it, my confession was news to me. To be honest, I hadn't thought about it until that moment. Although I enjoyed his company, it would be wrong to keep him there.

"Fine. Let's do it your way then, but if I end up dead, I'm going to be so pissed at you. And if I haunt you…"

"Don't say things like that!" *It's not good to tempt fate*, I thought but didn't say. Tina Louise used to make macabre statements like that. She'd threatened to haunt me a few times, too, but that was before. She never did. Losing Chloe wasn't an option. Not on my watch. "If you're ready, we'll go back up. We can't run this time. We've got to face it. It's time to take our house back. You with me?"

She jutted her chin out defiantly and rose from the couch with her camera in hand. "If you're game, I'm game. Let's do this, Tamara."

"Great," I said as we headed back upstairs to confront the Grim Reaper. For whatever reason, her description stuck in my mind. It was an apt name for the hooded figure. The only thing that was missing was a sickle. "Stay close," I whispered as we cleared the steps, and I flicked the light off. We were once again standing in complete darkness in the second-floor hallway.

Time to get this party started.

12

KEVIN

Nobody questioned me when I returned to the office with a stack of paperwork. Technically, I was supposed to keep quiet about my cases, but I was eager to talk to someone about them, and Tamara Garvey. Two other deputies were in the break room, the shift about to change, but I didn't see hide nor hair of Sheriff Jarvis. It felt like everyone knew I was working the cold case files and gave me a wide berth. I'd never been singled out for such a task, so I wasn't sure how much my involvement in this special assignment would stir the pot.

I had never been one to get involved in office politics, and I didn't want to start now. I waved goodbye to Willie Mae as I hung up the keys to the patrol car and exited the office. I was only a few days into this investigation, and I was extremely frustrated. Annie Hensley's friends either didn't want to share information or they didn't know anything.

No, Annie wasn't dating anyone when she died.

No, Annie wasn't on drugs or involved in anything illegal.

No. No. No.

How did this professional woman with no personal life and no ties to anything illegal end up dead by Black Snake Creek?

I'd managed to track down an ex-boyfriend of hers, but he wasn't much help either. He hadn't seen Annie for a few months before her death, so it wasn't much of a lead. I ran his alibi and verified there was no possible way he was anywhere in or around Crystal Springs on the night of her murder. He was in another part of the country so if that wasn't a rock-solid alibi, I didn't know what was.

I needed to get my mind on something else, and the unexpected invitation from Tamara Garvey fit the bill. I'd been dying to get back in the house, so I sure wasn't going to pass this opportunity up. Not to mention, I was pretty handy with a crowbar. Of course, I planned on keeping as much information to myself as possible. I'd give her a few crumbs about past deaths around the Ridaught Plantation for her book or her amusement. I couldn't be sure which.

Tamara said six o'clock, but I was ready to go at five-thirty. I killed some time drinking half a beer before heading out. I thought I should have worn my uniform and not blue jeans. Was she expecting Deputy Patrick or plain old Kevin Patrick? She'd offered me dinner, so I imagined this was technically a social call. I couldn't go empty-handed.

What did you bring to a dinner invitation? Flowers? No. That would indicate this was a date, and it wasn't.

I sailed into Edward's Pharmacy and patrolled the aisles

for a suitable thanks-for-the-dinner-invitation gift. I didn't think wine or beer would be appropriate. Not everyone drank alcohol. It was a possibility Tamara Garvey was in recovery or not a drinker, and if I brought her booze, it would mean I was enabling her. I couldn't have that on my conscience.

I'd watched too much Dr. Phil lately, I thought. I was overthinking this.

I decided to bring something every woman loved: candy. Not chocolate because that was too date-ish, but hard candy. Candy would be perfect, I hoped. Or not. Maybe I'd just keep the candy. I wouldn't know for sure until I got there. Everything about this dinner was weird. I left the pharmacy with my candy and headed to the Ridaught Plantation.

Tamara Garvey, a woman of mystery. Nothing had come up for her name, and I'd done a statewide search. I wanted to run her name through the national database but needed a good reason to do so. I couldn't just pick up the phone and ask the feds to check out a prankster.

I shook my head at my own thoughts as I pulled into the driveway. As I climbed up the steps to the front door, I took in the view. It was a beautiful old place, but it was more like a movie set than a home. Miss Garvey must have some money stashed away if she planned on making this place an actual home. Before I could tap the knocker, the door opened. I expected Tamara to step out, but there was no one there. An odd sort of breeze rushed past me, fluttering my hair and my shirt. Then nothing.

"Hi, I'm a few minutes early," I offered, but there was no one there. Was this another joke? "Hello?"

I heard music playing in the distance and footsteps thumping my way. Tamara came to the door, wiping her hands on a blue and white checkered kitchen towel. "Hi, come in. Did Chloe leave the door open like that?"

"Probably didn't close it good. Nice to see you. I brought you these." I handed her the sad plastic bag of hard candy. I felt like a cheap-ass bringing candy to a dinner.

"Oh. Candy? Halloween candy, too. Great," she said with a big smile. "I didn't make a dessert."

Idiot. Hard candy? Smooth.

She welcomed me inside. It was my second visit to the Ridaught Plantation, and this time I wasn't on the job. It was a work in progress with sparse, dated furniture, but the place had some great things going for it. Hardwood floors, antique trim that appeared to be in good shape. Not bad for a location that had been left empty for so long.

We paused in a cramped living room. "This is Chloe and her friend Trey. Guys, this is Deputy Patrick." The teenagers glanced up from their phones, glanced at each other and went back to texting, or whatever they were doing. "Chloe?"

"Hey," Chloe said as she put her phone down. "Nice to meet you, Deputy."

"Please call me, Kevin. I'm off the clock. Nice to see you, Trey. How's your dad doing? Feeling better?" Trey paled and shrugged.

"I guess. I haven't seen him in a while. Have you?"

Shoot. *Inappropriate, Kevin.*

The senior Trey Burger might not appreciate me putting his business out on the street. It was easy to assume the newbies wouldn't know all the small-town secrets.

Like, Trey's father was a notorious huffer and had been for years. Huffing was a poor man's way of getting high. People with his kind of addiction breathed in spray paint, gas fumes, you name it. How the man managed to have a family was beyond me. From what I knew of his activities, he was rarely sober, and whatever brain cells he had left, he'd killed breathing in his favorite chemicals. Big waste of a life. Which was bad for Trey Junior.

"Sorry. I just meant...sorry."

"Hey, it's not a big deal. I better take this call." I didn't hear the phone ring, but Trey put the phone to his ear and walked out of the house, leaving the front door open slightly. Nobody followed him, and I didn't think anyone noticed he'd left. Chloe had followed Tamara into the kitchen. I hadn't meant to run the kid off. Cold chills covered my body, but the sensation only lasted a few seconds.

"Did Trey leave?" Tamara asked as she stepped back in the hallway.

"Not sure. He went outside. He said something about a phone call."

"Come on, Kevin. I made a salad. Are you hungry? I hope so since I think it's going to be just you and me. Chloe's got something to do."

"Yes, ma'am. I rarely cook for myself, so a home-cooked meal is a treat."

"Don't get excited. It's a salad, so no home-cooking."

"If it didn't come from a drive-thru or out of a can, it's home-cooking. I'm sure even your worst dinner would be better than mine. Not that yours will be bad. As you can see, I don't get many dinner offers."

She sat at a small table, her hands fidgeting nervously in front of her. "Oh, I don't believe that. What would you like to drink? I've got cola, tea, and bottled water."

"Water is fine with me, ma'am."

"It's 'Tamara,' not ma'am, Kevin." After pouring herself a glass of tea and handing me a bottle of water, she sat with me. I guessed we were waiting for the teenagers, but I was starving. "Any word on our mystery screamer? Any other reports?"

"No, but I haven't been in the office much the past few days, Tamara. Have you seen your neighbor lately?" I cracked open the water.

"No, but I'm sure she'll be here for the party."

"How do you like living here? It's a big place. I think I could fit four of my apartments in here."

"It's huge," she told me. "Really huge. You should see my power bill. But it's Chloe's place, her family home. I'm here for her. It's only temporary. For me, at least."

"I'm sorry to hear that. Must be nice except for the occasional disembodied scream."

"That's what I wanted to talk to you about. As I mentioned, I am a writer. I thought it might be a good project to write something about the place, even just for Chloe. She doesn't know much about her family. They built this place, and maybe it could give us some clues about the screamer."

"I'm not sure I follow unless you're suggesting the history of this house is related to your prankster. You know, come to think of it, there are a lot of people who think this place should stay empty. It could be someone wants you to leave. Small-minded of them, but it's certainly possible."

With a weak smile, she sipped her tea. "I don't want to believe that, but it's possible. It happened again, Kevin. We heard it again last night. I went to investigate, but I haven't found a clue as to who is screaming. It is terrifying to hear, but I guess you know that. It almost doesn't sound human."

"An animal, maybe?" Even as I made the suggestion, I didn't believe it. I knew what screaming sounded like, human screaming. This particular example was more bloodcurdling but a hundred percent living person. Where was she going with this? "Possums do make strange noises. Squirrels. Lots of creatures burrow into walls and floors, and camp out in attics."

"You think it was a squirrel? No offense, but I question your policing skills if you don't want to admit that was a person and not a marsupial."

"I think the word you're looking for is 'rodent,'" I joked, trying to dissuade her from becoming even more intense and focused. Tamara had an opinion, and she very much wanted to tell me about it.

She leaned back in her chair with her head tilted at a pretty angle. "Oh, that's definitely not the word I was thinking."

"Hey, I'm going to my room. Trey is gone. Later," Chloe remarked as she shot me a go-to-hell look. I didn't know the teenager well, but I knew that look. Her foster mom wore it quite frequently.

"You might want to stick around, Chloe. We're about to break into the attic. After I show Kevin here my photos of the silver. Don't you want to see what's up there?"

Chloe uncrossed her arms and shoved her hands deep into her baggy jeans. "Count me out. Try not to tear the house apart." To Tamara, she said, "You should know Joey is back. He's in your room."

Tamara shifted in her seat, and her face paled. She didn't make eye contact with me, but she knew I was watching. "Okay, thanks. Can't you keep an eye on him for a while?"

"Not a chance, Tamara. He's your responsibility. Not mine."

"Fine." Some sort of strange silent exchange passed between them. They stared at each other as if daring one another to speak and tell a secret—a secret I needed to know. My suspicious mind ran in a thousand directions. Chloe disappeared, and I heard her footsteps echoing up the stairs and down the second-floor hall. Clearly, Tamara Garvey was having a difficult time here. I couldn't help but feel sympathy for her.

I thought about offering her some untested advice but then decided it best to keep my mouth shut. After a few awkward moments, she reached inside the purse on the chair beside her and pulled out her cell phone. "I have to show you something, Kevin. When you left the other day, well, more stuff happened. It's going to seem crazy when you see it, but this is no joke. No joke at all. Please, try to have an open mind."

"Joey? You didn't tell me you had a roommate. Maybe I should talk to him."

Tamara slid the phone toward me, and I picked it up with an uncommitted shrug. "You have to see this, Kevin."

I wasn't prepared.

13

TAMARA

The house popped as the temperature dropped outside. This house made noises a lot whenever the weather changed, even a few degrees. I remembered I promised this guy a meal, so rather than sitting around waiting for him to throw my phone back at me and walk out, I decided to dish up the salad and chicken. Chloe left us alone, clearly peeved her friend had made a hasty exit, but she wasn't aggravated enough to tell me why. I didn't understand her deal, talking about Joey in front of Kevin. He was bound to ask about him again.

I wondered if "He's my roommate, but he's also a ghost" would work.

I was sure that would go over great. How long until Joey appeared in the kitchen and I had to pretend he wasn't there? "Do you like ranch dressing, or would you prefer Italian?"

"No dressing, please. This was filmed here? At this table?"

"Yes," I answered as I brought the salad and a healthy

slice of chicken breast to the table with some silverware. "Right here. Same morning you came. Right after you left, in fact."

"Do you mind if I send a copy of these to my inbox?"

"Go right ahead." I sat in my chair and poked at my tiny salad with the fork, but I didn't have much of an appetite. "The only reason I showed you those pictures and video is to prove to you... Well, I don't know what it proves except there can be only one explanation. This is paranormal. There's no way all this silver was brought into this kitchen without me hearing or seeing anything in less than ten minutes. Look at the way it is assembled. Forks pointing out, up to the ceiling. Some of the spoons are twisted, and I have no idea where that cup came from." I pointed to the cup on the counter. I didn't want to touch the thing.

"No offense, Tamara, but how do I know that?"

"What?" I paused in mid-poke. "You're joking, right? Who the hell would make this up? I'm not trying to sell the house or drum up a media circus for personal gain. I know you don't know me, but that's not me. I'm trying to make a good impression on Crystal Springs, for Chloe's sake. I need someone to believe me and help me figure out what and why and how to put a stop to it." He sighed and appeared slightly off his game. Strange how talk of a few ghosts did that to folks. Especially overly confident folks like Kevin Patrick. Why did I feel as if I needed to prove something to this man?

Before I could delve too deeply into the psychology of my stab at friendship with Deputy Patrick, Joey sailed past the door, and I mean sailed. His nonexistent feet didn't touch the ground. He kind of glided but really fast, as if he was being pulled on an invisible sled or some sort of weird cartoon character. His head was slung back, and his neck stretched slightly, giving the illusion that centrifugal force was pulling him against his will. Just when I thought it was over Joey sailed by again only this time, he held a different pose. He even gave me a thumbs-up sign. Joey's wide-eyed facial expressions would normally make me laugh. His hand was over his mouth as he gawked at the back of Kevin Patrick. Yes, he was doing his best to get me classified as crazy. Didn't he understand what was at stake here? Poor, confused Kevin glanced over his shoulder at the open doorway, but Joey had vanished. I knew he wouldn't be gone long. He couldn't help himself. Joey was an A-Number-One cut-up and an attention hog.

There was another man in the house, and a handsome one too. I hadn't thought this through at all. I should have invited him for coffee somewhere instead of bringing him here.

"What is it?"

"Nothing," I said as I poked at my salad again. I wasn't hungry in the slightest.

"It must be something. You were laughing."

"No, I wasn't," I denied as I popped a cherry tomato into my mouth. He shrugged noncommittally and began chowing down. A big chunk of awkward silence passed between us.

"This has to be hard for you, raising a kid who's not your own. She's definitely got a chip on her shoulder about this arrangement. Taking on the challenge of raising a teenager and bringing this old place back to life is a lot for anyone to attempt. I give you credit for trying. Most people would have walked away from both of them, I think."

"I'm not most people," I snapped back. "You can't tell me you've seen anything like that photo. It's unsettling, even for me, and I know something about the subject of the paranormal. I've been on dozens of investigations, and I have never seen this kind of display. That scream and the disembodied voice aren't good signs either."

Kevin slid his plate to the side and leaned on his hands as he studied me. "You were a paranormal investigator? How did you get into that?" Oh, damn. Now he was investigating me.

"A friend got me interested in the subject. Chloe's mother, actually. Her name was Tina Louise. We worked together for a while, but I had no idea she owned a place like this, and she didn't leave me any information about it. Now I hear it's called the Ridaught Dead House? What has she gotten us into?" I was whispering as if that would stop Joey from popping in.

"People like to romanticize historical places like this one."

"'The Dead House' doesn't sound romantic to me. Why? Why is it called that, Kevin?"

His eyes trained on me, he ignored my question and asked one of his own. "People tend to die around here, in the house or on the grounds. Like the murder I'm investigating. She died near the creek. But you tell me. What do you think is going on, Tamara? Be honest. I feel like you want to tell me something, but I'm not sure what it is. Just tell me."

Joey's head peeked around the doorway, but there were

no shenanigans this time. His face was serious, worried, and focused on our conversation. He was wearing his usual striped polo shirt, the tight black clothes gone. His hair was not poking up, and he was fading.

"Tamara?"

With a half-smile, I momentarily toyed with the idea of doing just that, but the street-smart side of me warned not to take such drastic measures. We weren't quite friends yet, although I wanted to be. I needed an ally, and one that had information. Clearly, Joey didn't want me to do this. He slowly shook his head and then vanished in a fine mist. His sad expression worried me more than I could have imagined. Maybe I was making too much of all this.

"I think the place might be haunted. It sure has all the hallmarks, but I want to do my due diligence. Tell me about this murder. When did this happen? Recently?"

"Annie Hensley was her name. She was murdered years ago, but no one was ever charged. She's a cold case I'm working. She was a nursing assistant and worked at a senior home nearby. It's closed now. There was no reason for her to meet such a horrible end. She wasn't assaulted or robbed, and Annie didn't have any enemies. I have a lot of whys and no answers."

"I didn't know you worked on cold cases. That must be challenging. Where did she die on the property? You said the creek? Back that way?"

He shifted in his seat again, clearly put off I hadn't answered his questions and I had plenty of my own. "Yes, she died by Black Snake Creek, about half a mile from here. Have you been down to the creek yet?"

"Interesting," I whispered as I bit my lip, remembering

seeing the apparition fleeing from the house. She hadn't been alone. I wondered what had happened to the woman in the wheelchair. I glanced at the doorway, but there was no sign of Joey. I could feel him sighing somewhere nearby. It must have been an audible sigh because Kevin turned again in search of the source of the sound. Music began blaring from Chloe's room, and I could hear her stomping around. "No thoughts about the silver?"

"Not at this time. I'll have to get back to you on that, although I'm sure you know things you aren't telling me."

That brought a smile to my face. I liked being a woman with a touch of mystery. "Never forget that. You say you brought a crowbar? Feel like breaking into the attic?"

"Yes. I'll go get it, but you haven't answered my question. What do you think is happening here? Why am I really here, Tamara Garvey?"

"To help me find out why there's a screamer in Chloe's family home and poltergeist-like activity is occurring here in this kitchen. Who was the ghost woman I saw from the second-floor window? She was a blonde woman wearing a nurse's uniform. And what the hell is the hooded figure we're seeing at the end of the hallway."

Put that in your pipe and smoke it, Deputy Patrick.

His mouth drew up into a smile but quickly faded. He knew I wasn't joking. At least he didn't call me crazy or mock me.

He didn't interrogate me but instead said matter-of-factly, "I guess I better go get that crowbar."

TAMARA

If my confession shook Deputy Kevin Patrick, he didn't let on. Then again, I didn't know him all that well. He could be quaking in his boots or quietly classifying me as a nut job. Kevin Patrick was a complete and utter mystery, and I liked that. He was here, and that had to mean something. Or he could be planning to call an asylum later to ask if they had an extra butterfly net for one screwed up burlesque dancer. Ex-dancer.

What choice did I have? He asked me what I thought and I told him. I glanced down the hallway as I waited for Kevin to return with the crowbar. I didn't like being here. This spot was about where the hooded figure had been standing, all shrouded in blackness and full of hate. I shivered as I glanced over my shoulder. No one was there, alive or dead. Chloe remained camped out in her room, and I prayed Joey stayed away until Kevin left. He was not someone I could explain.

Meet my dead best friend. His name is Joey.

At least Joey was okay and was here.

"Got it," Kevin said as he came bounding up the steps. Funny, I didn't even hear the front door open. I must have been lost in my thoughts. I did that sometimes.

"Great. May I give it a shot?" I asked as I held out my hand expectantly.

He tilted his head as if I needed a butterfly net. "Really?"

"Yes, I think I can handle a crowbar, Deputy. It's just a lever, right?"

"Right. Pardon me." Without a trace of disbelief, he handed the metal tool to me, and I went to work on the wooden door. Or tried to get to work on it. Getting the tip of the crowbar into the door seam proved a challenge. Whoever put the door in knew what they were doing because it was set as straight and even as you could humanly place it.

After a few minutes of me sweating and swearing, he said, "The wood must have swollen. It happens when there's high humidity. The funny thing about these old houses is they shift around a lot." I wiped the sweat from my brow and handed him the crowbar.

"Let's see what you can do then. I'm spent." I wasn't joking in the slightest. I didn't want to say it, but it felt almost like an invisible force was working against me. I smiled victoriously when Kevin didn't do any better than I had with the dang thing.

Chloe stood in the hallway with her hands on her hips as if she were a parent catching two naughty teenagers breaking into the liquor cabinet. "Y'all suck at breaking into places."

I answered her in a calm, even voice. "Care to give a try, smarty pants? The attorney won't call me back, and we need to see what's in there. Deputy Patrick wants to make sure it is safe, is all," I said confidently as I widened my eyes at him. He wasn't great at reading social cues.

"I'd rather watch you tear the place up."

"We need to make sure no one is hurt up here. Those screams were pretty loud." Deputy Patrick sweated and grunted as he tried to jimmy the door open.

Chloe snorted at our stupidity. "Do you think I believe that? If you were concerned about someone being trapped in the attic, Deputy, you would have broken in last time. What's really going on?"

"Getting into this room is the next step in investigating this activity. I will personally fix whatever we break, I swear," I said in a calm voice.

"Why can't we just wait for the key? You're going to tear the plantation to pieces, Tamara. Between your half-assed renovation and the cop tearing the door down, there won't be anything left standing." That was harsh. I didn't believe that Chloe was concerned about the door coming down, but she was clearly upset with me. It must have been because of whatever passed between Kevin and Trey earlier. She was temperamental, and I didn't understand her.

"Is there a problem with me getting into the attic? Something you want to tell me?" Kevin asked as he turned away from his task. He hadn't made any progress. The door did not want to open. I didn't like his tone, but Chloe could fend for herself. Of that, I had no doubt.

"I don't have anything to hide from anyone. For your information, I've never been in the attic. So, whatever you're suggesting, you can stick it where the..."

As we all stood there, involved in our disagreement, the attic door suddenly clicked open and squeaked heavily on its hinges.

We watched in silence as the door began to open wider. A small cloud of dust poofed into the hallway as if something passed, but there was no one there. How on earth? "Did you do that?" I asked Kevin in a whisper.

"You know I didn't. I've got the crowbar right here." He looked from me to Chloe. How could the door come open like that? The only explanation I could come up with would be that Joey had opened it. That had to be it. Chloe was frozen and was staring at the open door. Kevin put his crowbar down, leaning it against the wall, and walked into the now open room. No how, no way was I leaving the crowbar behind. I reached for it and clutched it like a bat.

Chloe came in behind me. We stood just inside the door and took in the view. I've heard of cluttered attics before, but this took the cake. It looked like a freaking antique store and flea market on steroids. The attic was huge, much larger than I had imagined, and it had a bit of everything. I saw dressmaker's dummies, a creepy, oversized dollhouse, rocking chairs, a rocking horse, and loads of wooden crates with mysterious scribbles on the sides. Those were just the first things I noticed. There were also shelves laden with dolls, toys, and other strange items.

I saw a drum-banging monkey toy. I have hated those things ever since I saw that Mia Farrow movie. That had to go.

There were more boxes than I could count. Some were modern cardboard boxes, and some looked wooden and much older. There were even stacks of suitcases. What wasn't visible was any record player or any wires or anything that would lead me to believe the screams we heard came from this room.

"Holy cow." That was all Chloe could say as she walked through the jumbled aisles, examining her family's collected items. It was a dust-laden legacy.

"Satisfied?" I asked Kevin in a whisper as I stayed close to him. He was working his way through the maze but didn't answer me. His eyes fell on the same thing mine did.

Resting against a nearby wall was an empty wheelchair. The back was turned toward us, and I clearly read CRYSTAL RIVER HOME on the back.

Unless I was mistaken, which was a distinct possibility, it was the same wheelchair I'd seen Annie Hensley pushing as she fled the plantation the night the Screamer showed up. I pushed past Kevin and hurried toward it. It looked like the right one, with dingy white leather strapping and steel handles. The wheels were metal but a bit rusty.

"I saw this. I saw this chair, and the ghost nurse was pushing it away from the house."

"Let's just keep our heads on straight. When you say ghost, you mean someone who looked like Annie Hensley? Not an actual ghost, right? Because I don't know if I believe in that sort of thing. I am a law enforcement officer, remember?"

"Be that as it may, I saw Annie Hensley's ghost, Kevin. She was running from the house, pushing this wheelchair. Or one very like it," I added in a whisper, but I needn't have worried. Chloe ignored us both and seemed to have completely forgotten she was mad at me. She was busy digging through boxes looking for God knew what.

Kevin didn't ask me any more questions, and I decided to keep my mouth shut and my thoughts to myself. After a bit of searching and digging around the attic, I finally said to him, "Are you satisfied now? There is no wiring system up here. We haven't been pranking you or anyone, for that matter. Whatever or whoever is screaming in this house isn't hiding up here."

"Then how do you explain it?"

I could see he wasn't flirting with me, and he wasn't joking. Chloe rolled her eyes and said, "Whatever. At least you didn't break the door." She stomped out of the attic with a few items in her arms, and I heard her clomp back down the hall to her room and then the door slam behind her.

"I think you should leave, Deputy Patrick. I let you see the attic, and you still don't want to give me the benefit of the doubt. That's pretty short-sighted. You're busy trying to bust me doing something illegal when I'm not doing a damn thing wrong. Except raise a teenager. I'm doing it pretty poorly, but I don't think that's a crime. Or am I mistaken?"

Kevin wiped the sweat off his forehead with the back of his hand. "Annie Hensley was a nurse and an all-around good person, according to her friends. She died at Black Snake Creek, which runs just behind this house. She was murdered, Tamara, and here's something most people don't know. Annie might have been the victim of a serial killer. I shouldn't be telling you that detail, but since you let me in your attic, I owe you something."

I closed the box beside me. There wasn't much inside except a stack of old newspapers. How many of these boxes were full of junk like that? This attic could be a fire hazard. "I didn't let you in here," I reminded him. "The door opened on its own. Remember?"

Kevin ran his hands through his hair and picked up his crowbar, which I'd laid on a nearby box. "Oh, excuse me. The ghost let me in here, and it's a screaming ghost, terrifying the neighborhood. That will look great in a report. Listen, thanks for the invitation. I plan on doing my best to seek justice for Annie. Thanks for dinner, and thanks for everything."

"Well, I guess we're done here then," I said, feeling a little stung from his heated words. Shouldn't one of us break out the curse words? This was the politest argument I'd ever been in.

"I guess so. Have a nice evening."

"Thanks, I will." He walked out of the attic and headed down the stairs without turning back, then left the house without a word. To say it was anticlimactic was an understatement. Whatever connection we had been making was sure as hell over.

At least I knew the ghost's name. I did find out that much. Now I had to go in search of Joey. Maybe he'd have some information for me, and I could thank him for opening the door. I closed the attic door behind me and tried the knob. It wasn't locked now, which was weird. I paused outside Chloe's door but couldn't hear anything. She probably had her headphones on.

I went back to my bedroom, but Joey was nowhere to be found. I called his name a few times, hoping he'd show up, but he didn't. With growing frustration at both the men in my life, I went to my office and decided to open the computer and send off a few emails. I thought about emailing Quinton. I wasn't sure about opening the door to that two-timing jerk again, but I didn't have much choice. I didn't have anyone else to turn to. Tina Louise was gone along with all her connections. I mean, I had a few but not like my late bestie. Quinton might not even answer me, but I decided to give it a shot.

A few minutes later, I was adding attachments and sending an email to my ex-boyfriend. I also sent him my address for research purposes only, which I indicated politely in the body of the text, but I decided to leave off my cell phone number. With shaky fingers, I clicked send.

It was done, for better or for worse. *Go to bed, Tamara. You're delirious.*

I closed down the computer and went to bed.

ANNIE HENSLEY

1987

When I woke up, the world was a different place. I expected to see hospital machines, maybe bright lights above me, and fluorescent lights, the kind I worked under every day. I belonged in a hospital because I'd been hurt. I could feel the pain in my head and my face and all over.

"Hello?" I whispered, but nobody was in these woods. I couldn't even say how I'd gotten there.

Confusion. Sadness. Anger.

I felt more than I thought, more than I could reason. I had many feelings, but reasoning proved difficult. I'd always been a reasonable person.

"Is there anyone here?" I sobbed as I began to travel through the dark woods. I breezed past bushes and trees. I moved quickly, so quickly it startled me. I wanted to get out. I had to get out of here.

He'd been after me—the man in white. What was his name?

Flashes of his face, wolfish and dark, appeared before me, but I swatted the memory away. I did not want to remember. I did not want to know.

I walked through the endless woods. They were so dark and so thick I could see nothing, not even the hand in front of my face. I had to keep moving, or he would find me. He would find me and hurt me again.

No! No more, please! No more!

The pain returned, and my hand rubbed my head. There had been blood everywhere.

Marjorie! I had to find Marjorie. My poor friend was lost and far from home. She'd gone to the house, the big house where the ghosts lived. That was what Marjorie used to say. Ghosts. At the house. What was the place called? Why was my memory so terrible?

I moaned as I glided through the woods. I was gliding, not walking. No branches slapped me, and no vines cut me.

My name is Annie Hensley. That is my name. Annie. I am Annie. I need to find Marjorie.

It was so dark. I moaned again.

Then I saw a light, a bright light. It shone through the woods like a warm pink spotlight. It was lovely.

I began to travel toward it.

If I could get to the light, I would find Marjorie. I would find what I needed. I could escape these dark woods and the man in white. Paul, that was his name.

His name was Paul.

I moved even more quickly toward the light.

No. I can't leave her. Marjorie, I have to make sure she's safe. I stepped away from the light even though I wanted to run toward it. I couldn't leave her behind. Not with Paul. He would hurt her.

As if the light heard my argument, as if it knew my thoughts, it faded away.

I was surrounded by darkness again.

CHLOE

I was back in my own room and determined to hold my ground. As fierce as I pretended to be, the image of the hooded reaper standing at the end of the hallway haunted me. There was no denying it had a profound effect on me. I even saw the thing in my dreams, but I did my best to put it out of my mind. This was my house. For real. The Ridaught Plantation belonged to my mother and her mother before her. This house was the only thing left of my mom, and I wasn't going to abandon it. I would not go quietly because of an apparition.

I wasn't sure, but Joey could have been to blame for the entity's appearance. I didn't think it was possible it was actually Joey, I mean, he ran out ahead of me and had been equally terrified by it. Tamara wanted to help him, but I kind of felt as if she were out of her element. She'd only been a paranormal hobbyist, not a professional paranormal investigator. She might have seen every *Ghost Hunters* episode known to man, but that didn't make a person an expert on the subject. I preferred *Ghost Adventures,* but that didn't mean I was an expert either.

I texted Trey one more time, but he didn't answer. I didn't know what the deputy said to him, but it had put the fear of God in him. I didn't know Trey that well, but I liked the guy. I'd try to text him again later. I put the crystals Lynn had given me on the dresser and some on the night-stand. They were supposed to repel negative energy. Black tourmaline was my absolute favorite. We'd had an unsteady friendship until we started talking about crystals. I wasn't even sure how the conversation came up except I was hanging out by Trey's locker and so was she. It didn't take me long to figure out they were cousins and best friends. I liked her too. I would proceed carefully with the friendship, though. I'd been burned by new "friends" before.

I wanted to get back into the attic to take a look around. It had to be Mom who opened the door, so I could explore her things. I had my big flashlight, and for some reason, I felt compelled to bring some of the black crystals with me. I had gotten into crystals last year, and I believed in their ability to influence the environment. I was hoping to avoid negative entities, so hematite seemed the right tool for the job. After checking my phone one last time and seeing I had no messages, I decided to get on with it. The only bad thing about checking out the attic was I had to go past the spot where the hooded figure hung out. Every time I thought about it, the memory gave me the chills. It couldn't be anything other than the Grim Reaper. Why would he be at the Ridaught Plantation? I wasn't even sure what Grim Reapers do.

Now that the door to the attic had been opened, I was dying to explore the place, and without Tamara and Kevin squabbling like an old married couple. I had to go. A strange compulsion drew me back to examine the contents. I wanted to look in every box and every nook and cranny. With my big flashlight in one hand and my crystals in the other, I walked into the attic and closed the door behind me. The click of the latch made me feel somewhat secure. It was always a good feeling to know no one could sneak up behind you. No living person, anyway.

Although there were tons of things to look at, and some obviously creepy and interesting items. I was drawn to the steamer trunks on the left side of the attic. I knew exactly who they belonged to. Those had to be my mother's old traveling trunks. I had wondered where they'd gone. Did Tamara know they were here? Was she trying to keep them from me?

Those trunks were like treasure boxes. Mom kept her expensive performance gowns in them, the ones I was never allowed to touch. Sometimes she unlocked them and shared her treasures with me. Such exquisite things.

As I drew closer, I saw a small cedar box and opened it. It was a neat box full of costume jewelry and the pieces were really old, but not my mother's stuff. I closed the jewelry box and set it aside. It wasn't what I was looking for. Someone must have stuffed it here at some point.

I recognized a trunk that was familiar. Luckily the lock was missing. I knelt in front of it as I rubbed my hands over the dirty lid. Yes, this was Mom's. I would recognize those old stickers anywhere. Funny Tamara didn't even notice them. *Mom! I miss you so much!*

Tears filled my eyes when I opened the lid. It was filled with my mother's things—two of her beautiful gowns, along with hats and feather boas and all of the beaded undergarments. They would be my treasures now.

In her day, Mom had been a star in her own right. Not a stripper as some would say, but a burlesque dancer. She always described herself as an artist. It was funny how as I got older, I didn't regret or resent her profession. What I did resent was that she never made time for me. I hated that Mom put those beautiful things and all of those experiences ahead of me. I loved her completely, yet I had not been enough. The horrible irony was, she died on the way to see me. Maybe if she'd stayed away, she'd still be alive. But then someone else's mom would have been killed by that drunk driver.

Someone else…

I lifted the dark green gown from the trunk and held it close, praying I would catch a whiff of her perfume. I breathed in deeply, but I could not smell her.

I miss you, Mom.

What would she think about me living here? I was pretty sure she had mentioned it when I was young, but I'd never been here before, and my grandmother never wanted to talk about the "Ridaught Place," as she referred to it. She had a healthy respect for supernatural things, and I think that was where I inherited her practical approach to the paranormal. All bets were off now. The family home was a strange place, but it was mine.

Mom, I wish you were here, I thought. *I know it's possible for you to come back because you talk to Joey. I know you can come back. Why won't you come to me?*

I focused my thoughts and waited for a response, but I heard nothing.

With a sigh, I clutched the green gown before moving on to the rest of the items. There were postcards. I waved the flashlight beam on the faint writing, but it was difficult to see. Maybe if I had my glasses. I thought I was too young to be this blind. Not having the patience to examine them closely, I set the postcards on the floor beside me and continued to sort through the trunk. There was nothing else to see, just the other dress and accessories. I turned my attention to a trunk next to this one. It wasn't my mom's, or at least I didn't recognize it, but I was curious.

Moving the rusty latch, I opened it and found a bunch of newspapers. There were wrapped items but nothing special, just some Christmas ornaments. Each ornament was hand-painted and elegantly crafted. I thought they were porcelain. There was a bell, a silver bell with a fading red ribbon. I would have to remember these things at Christmas. I wondered who all this belonged to. I knew what I was going to wear for Halloween—my mom's dress.

I'd been wracking my brain for just the right costume, and this was it. As I stood up to stretch my back, I clutched the dress to my chest. I heard a sound behind me. It sounded like the scrabbling of rodent feet across a nearby board. Then I heard it again on the other side of me. The sound was too loud to be mice or rats.

I waved my flashlight in the direction of the sound and noticed a small burst of dust rising from the floor as if something just ran past me.

"Joey? Is that you? Cut it out," I warned as the hair on the back of my neck rose. Then I felt a strange sensation, like I'd walked through a spider's web. It felt as if it covered my face and ears. I sputtered and yelped as I wiped my face with my hand, but I could find nothing. I furiously ran my fingers through my hair to make sure there wasn't some big-ass spider crawling all over me. Spiders were the worst. I waved the flashlight around, looking for the source of the spiderweb and completely forgetting about the scratching sound for a few seconds until I heard it again.

This time it was closer to the door.

Oh, my God! What if there was some kind of weird giant spider roaming around in the attic? There were hundreds of places for it to hide. I scrambled to my feet to investigate, then stood by the door and listened to the strange sounds.

Scramble, scramble. Scratch, scratch. It gave me chills.

I edged away from the door and the source of the sound as quickly and quietly as possible. To make matters worse, the spiderweb was back, and all over my body now. I felt like I was in a horror movie. How many times had I screamed at the television warning whoever was on screen not to turn their backs? I couldn't take my eyes off the attic door.

Keep walking. Count to ten. Breathe, girl.

Whatever was making the sound stopped, and the creepy spiderweb sensation subsided. I was still clutching the dress and the stack of postcards while waving my flashlight when something caught my eye. It wasn't in the attic, but a light in the yard. The sun had gone down hours ago, and there were no electric lights in the backyard, but there were several dull yellow lights that looked like candles. Who in the world would be walking around outside with candles? I turned off the flashlight and momentarily forgot my fear of spiders. I stepped closer toward the window, hoping not to be noticed by whoever was skulking around down there.

Something was not right. It was going on midnight, I guessed. I wondered if I should go tell Tamara. I decided against it, mostly because I didn't want to talk to her. I couldn't say why. I spent most of my time mad at her for no apparent reason other than she was here and my mother was not. That didn't make sense even to me, but it was what it was, as Trey liked to say.

I should've brought my phone. I'd left it by the trunk. It would've been nice to have pictures of what I saw. I retrieved it quickly and hurried out of the attic, surprised to find Joey hovering in the hallway. He was leaning against the wall, his arms crossed. His eyebrow was cocked up as if he had caught me doing something very naughty. To make his whole expression seem even more ridiculous, he was wearing a doo-rag on his head. He did love doo-rags. At least this one was from Tamara's shabby collection.

"Joey? Why are you always spying on me?"

"Why are you always such a snot? Nice dress, by the way."

"It comes naturally, I guess. Maybe I inherited it. Why don't you ask my mom the next time you see her? Now, if you don't mind..." I moved past Joey, ignoring his luminous face. He had forgotten to manifest his legs, which made him look ridiculous.

Joey's expression shifted, and he was as sad-looking as

any puppy. "Don't go out there. You're inviting trouble by going out there, Chloe."

"What do you know about what's out there? Did you have something to do with this?"

He faded but didn't vanish completely. "Do I look like I have something to do with any of that? I am in here, and they're out there. I want to keep it that way, but you keep poking the hornets' nest. You have to stop. They can see you and hear you. You're pulling them closer."

I whispered in surprise, "Me? So you know about the lights? Those lights are ghosts? What's going on, Joey?"

"I don't know. I try to avoid them. Please, don't go out there. They will see you if you go outside. Your light will draw everything in the neighborhood."

I rubbed my forehead as a headache threatened to blind me. "Have you lost your mind?"

"Yes. I lost my mind a long time ago. You are too bright, Chloe. If you wouldn't mind, how about toning it down a little so the rest of us can get some sleep?"

"That doesn't sound right. Meditation is supposed to stop that kind of thing from happening. Did you leave your head in the oven too long?"

His other eyebrow cocked up. "For most people, that's true. I mean, I'm a *Ghost Travelers and Dead Cases* fanboy. I know all about this stuff, and normally that's how it works. Do some meditation, sprinkle some water, apply some oil. That can help 'normal' people." He air-quoted "normal" to me. "But not you, Chloe. By stopping up the spigot, you attract more negativity. Like those lights. Those lights ain't nothing good, and there's more of them gathering around this place."

I didn't know what to say. How was that possible?

"I'm doing my best to help you, Chloe. I'm exhausted, but I am trying. You have to give me that."

"What about Mom? Have you seen her?" I asked as I leaned against the opposite wall.

"No, I haven't since the storm. But that is what I mean. The more you reach out to her, the more everything reaches back. She can't come here. She's banned by...I don't know what, but she can't be here!"

"You're here, though. Why can't she be here?"

"That's above my pay grade, sweetie. All I know is you are attracting all kinds of bugs, so whatever you have to do, do it. I'll do my best to push them back, but I'm flaming out and quick. Don't go out there." Joey vanished before I could interrogate him further. I decided against going outside in the middle of the night to confront candle-wielding strangers. Or ghosts. Or whatever was outside.

With a death grip on the dress and postcards, I ran to my room and turned on every light I had. Joey might get some rest, but I was never going to fall asleep.

Probably ever again.

17

TAMARA

I was exhausted but excited about the progress we'd made. The bottom floor of the Ridaught Plantation looked amazing, like Halloweentown meets a haunted house. It was like something out of a movie set, with plenty of scary touches but in a classy sort of way. I had no idea Chloe was so good at decorating and staging furniture and accessories. To think, I'd ignored all her advice on paint colors and the like when we moved in here. Note to self: Chloe has an eye for style.

I was impressed by her attention to detail and happily imagined her working with me in the future, maybe staging houses or even selling them. It was totally possible. If the whole book thing didn't work out. At this rate, I was never going to get the book written. I'd have to sell a few houses and soon. The good news was, several of my potential clients were coming to the party tonight.

Luckily, I had two properties to push, a small cottage on Lemon Tree Street and a little duplex on Birch. Both were dressed and ready to go, and I was sure I could turn them into cash. That is, if people would kindly attend my scheduled open houses.

Here at home, things had died down. It was as if Kevin and his crowbar had successfully repelled whatever was here, but that wasn't right. He hadn't even opened the door. Joey had said he didn't touch it and told me he didn't like that space. Sometimes the secret to ending paranormal activity was just to bring in the right personalities. Maybe that was all it took in this case.

Maybe the phantom Screamer just wanted the attic door open.

And I'm a college professor. I wasn't sure, but I was happy things had settled down. Once in a while, I got the feeling eyes were on me, but I didn't see or hear anything besides Joey. The three of us sank into our former routines, and I put my mind to pounding the pavement looking for buyers and writing a few paragraphs here and there. To be honest, my book had taken a strange turn, and I knew I'd have to make some revisions before I went any farther. Or maybe I wouldn't.

What publishing house would buy a haunted mystery? I had no idea, but then, I was a long way from being published.

I got a few friendly emails from Quinton asking for more details, but I backed off on getting him involved. I didn't even answer the last email. Joey and I had sunk back into our evening routine of watching *Ghost Hunters* reruns and gossiping on the couch. Chloe was back at school, the tornado damage having been repaired quickly. She and

Trey seem to be getting closer, but that was totally normal. He was a likable enough kid and occasionally, he brought his cousin around. Her name was Lynn, and she was an awkward ball of fun. I liked her. They usually hung around in the living room in the afternoon after school. It was fun having young people around.

We nailed those decorations. From the chandelier wafted silky spiderwebs, complete with tiny little green light-up spiders. There were also black lace fans scattered around, each glowing with a red light. A raven perched on the mantlepiece, with eyes that lit up when you walked past. Once in a while, it squawked, "Nevermore!"

The caterers had arrived and the sideboard in the dining room was covered with all kinds of creepy snacks, including finger sandwiches and various dips. I'd been getting phone calls all day. So many people were coming to this party. Apparently, the big shindig at the Dead House was the talk of the town, but there had been no RSVP from Kevin. I guess I knew where I stood. Maybe if the music played loud enough, he'd show up tonight in uniform. Strangely, I did like a man in uniform.

My phone dinged as another RSVP hit my notifications. My little bit of advertising on social media was paying off in a big way, but I couldn't pretend it was all my doing. I wasn't that skilled at marketing, but people were curious about this place. According to Chloe, half her school was coming, which was exciting.

Despite all the details we put into the display, Chloe wasn't happy with the results. She was a perfectionist. "It's missing something, Tamara. We need a better focal point.

That mirror isn't big enough. Tell you what...Trey, Lynn, and I will go back up to the attic and grab one of those old oil paintings. I'll put it over there."

"I think it looks great in here, Chloe, but if you think we need something else, go for it. After all this magic, I totally trust your judgment. You know, if you are looking for a summer job, I could use you. Staging a house isn't as easy as you make it look. I'd rather pay you than work with a staging company. They charge way too much. We could make a list of items, do the shopping, and store them in some of the spare rooms. What do you say, Chloe? Want to earn a few extra dollars?"

Chloe looked at me as if I lost my mind, and to accentuate her disgust, she rolled her eyes. "That sounds like a terrible idea. We don't need much, just the portrait and maybe one of those dressmaker's dummies. We could always dress the dummy up and make it look scary. Come on, Lynn, Trey, I'm going to need your help toting this picture. It looks like it weighs about a hundred pounds. I want you guys to see this place. It's unbelievable."

"Don't spend too much time up there. The guests will be arriving soon, and you're not even dressed," I called after them as the three teenagers bounded up the steps and went to the attic. I still had no idea what Chloe intended to come as since she had kept her costume completely secret.

My costume was lame. I had a bunch of Halloween-appropriate outfits, but none of them could be worn at our house party. I found a fuzzy headband and paired it with a black minidress that I hoped made me look like a cat. Or a cat-woman. A tailless cat-woman. At least I knew how to do makeup really well. I could knock out cat's eye eyeliner like nobody's business. Since we were alone on the bottom floor, Joey came out of my bedroom, and I almost died laughing.

"Is the coast clear?" he asked as he sauntered toward me. "Wow! What's new, pussy cat?"

"Ha!" I smothered another laugh at Joey, but he took it in stride. He was totally rocking a fitted—I mean *very* fitted —sailor costume. "Bravo, Joey!" To show me how much he loved his sailor costume, complete with white Popeye hat, he straightened his back and strolled down the hall like it was a runway. He was even wearing platform shoes, just high enough to make him look taller. At least he'd fully manifested his legs. He had trouble with that sometimes.

I never met a ghost who could do more than appear and reappear for a few moments, and that was often sporadic. Rarely were they friendly. Joey could interact with the physical world almost as well as I could, at least for short periods of time.

"Check it, girl. I'll be the hottest sailor in Crystal Springs."

"You look great, Joey. I mean, really great. How did you whip that up?"

"I've got my ways. Oh, and on second thought, what are you wearing? No, no, no. What happens if Deputy McHottie shows up and you look like a club ho? Why don't you wear one of those other outfits? The ones you have stashed in that closet back there. You know, the Little Red Riding Hood outfit is to die for."

"That's out of the question. That outfit is far too racy

for a PG party. Tell me, Popeye, do you plan to make an appearance tonight? Because if you do, you may want to tamp down the luminosity. You'll never blend in if you don't get that under control."

He groaned in response. "I'm trying, but it's hard. It's all Chloe's fault."

"What? What are you talking about?" I dropped my voice to a whisper as I glanced up the stairs, but nobody was coming down. Thankfully.

"She's a wildcard. I tell you, that girl has psychic powers. Secret gifts she's not telling you about," he said as he spun around one more time. I smiled supportively, all while silently praying he'd chicken out on showing up. I didn't take him seriously about Chloe. For some reason, those two had an active war going on. I couldn't figure them out.

"Besides, this light thing only happens when I get excited, and this is the most exciting thing that's happened to me in..." Joey's joyful expression vanished momentarily. I could see him struggling to remember when the last time he felt joyful and happy about something was. With all of my heart, I wanted to press him and push him to think a little harder, dig a little deeper, but he simply couldn't remember, and time wasn't on our side. I needed to distract him. I wanted him to be happy.

"You'll be the belle of the ball, Joey, but just a warning. Deputy McHottie is mine."

His beautiful grin returned as he smirked at me playfully.

"Oh, is that how you want to play it? Maybe I should break out my backup costume?" The radio in my bedroom began to play a hip-hop tune. Joey snapped his fingers and his costume changed in the twinkling of an eye. He was no longer wearing his rocking Popeye the Sailor Man costume, but a much more scandalous outfit, complete with a pair of micro shorts, a sailor crop top, a white hat, and white heels. It was ridiculous and also hilarious.

"Sorry, Sweet Cheeks, but not at this party. There will be kids present. It doesn't leave much to the imagination, does it?" I thought I heard footsteps upstairs. It sounded like the teens were returning. I glanced nervously at the door as Joey stood in front of the mirror and vogued before agreeing.

"You're probably right about this one. It's costume number one, then. Oh, well." The music stopped, and he straightened out his costume by smoothing it with his fingers. The doorbell rang before he could begin ransacking my closet. It was strange he didn't hear the guest approaching. Usually, he was better than a surveillance doorbell.

"Please don't tear my closet up. I don't have time to clean it up tonight."

"Oh, and you want to have everything tidy in case you get a little action? That's a relief. I was beginning to think you'd taken an oath of celibacy. I mean, it's ridiculous. I haven't seen one bare ass in there. Except yours. No offense, but you're not my type. You're cute and all, but I like my asses a bit brawnier."

I stomped my bare foot at him. "You've been looking at me naked?"

"Sweetie, I'm a ghost. I can't help but look. Trust me, it's nothing I haven't seen before."

I wasn't happy with his confession. "Oh, really? Well, don't do it again. I've got to answer the door. Stay out of trouble, please." I stormed out of the bedroom and closed the door behind me. Who could this be? They were an hour early.

Probably the DJ. He needed time to set up speakers and whatnot.

I put on a happy face. I don't know who I expected to see when I opened the door—maybe my nosy neighbor Linda Blabbermouth or hopefully Deputy Kevin Patrick—but the guy I saw was neither of those. This was no excited early bird come to take a peek inside the Ridaught Plantation. My guest was none other than professional ghost hunter and ex-boyfriend Quinton Lowell. Suddenly, Joey was just on the other side of the door peeking through the crack. I heard him squeal beside me as I stared in amazement at the sight of Quinton's tight shirt and even tighter pants.

"Hello, Pussy Cat. I see you got my email." If I was going to hear that corny name all night, I was going to change my outfit.

"What are you doing here?"

He dropped his overnight bag on the ground as though he was planning to spend the night. "In my last email, I told you I was coming down. I'm here to do a full investigation. That's what you want, right? Or is it just me you want?"

Quinton's attempts at charm didn't amuse me, especially since I could see his *Ghost Travelers* van in my driveway. The show had been canceled for a few years now. Talk about holding on to the past. It might add to the ambiance, I thought.

"I haven't been checking my email, but you're here, and I'm having a party. Um, please come in, Quinton. Bring your bag. I'll find a room for you. We'll have to talk about this later, though." Joey acted as if he were going to faint as I waved my hand at him to warn him to cool it.

This was going to be one hell of a Halloween party.

18

CHLOE

"Wow! Look at this crowd, Chloe! We're fifteen minutes away from kickoff, and it's already a legit party. Oh, crap. It looks like the Goth Bitches are here. Why did you invite them? They're four major pains in the ass. Cousins from hell. You don't know what you're in for."

Lynn bounced up and down on the seat beside me until she saw her nemeses gathering on the lawn. What did you call multiple enemies? I wasn't interested in getting into the weeds of past offenses with Lynn, but I sure as heck wasn't going to put up with any crap from fellow students. I'd definitely keep an eye out, but I planned on having fun. I peeked out the window, amazed at all the cars. Tamara wasn't prepared for this level of success, that was for sure. Trey had gone home to change, but he'd be coming back soon.

"Is that a real *Ghost Travelers* van? I can't believe it. I think it is! This is so legit! What if Ike and Doug are here? Do you know them?"

"Wrong show, and no. I don't know them. Tamara

might, though. Please help me with this dress. Can't put this off any longer. I can't wait to put on my costume."

Lynn clapped her hands joyfully. "Have you told Tamara yet?"

"It's my costume, so she doesn't get a say. I'm not a kid." I hadn't really thought about what she would think about seeing me in this dress. Lynn's phone began going off, and she got up to stare at her text message. I wasn't great at reading faces, but she'd gotten bad news.

"Shoot. I've got to go home, Chloe. I have something to do. I'm sorry to go, but I have to. I'll try to come back later this evening."

"What? But the party is about to get started. I know you want to be here. Everything okay at home, Lynn?" I was floored. My friend didn't share many details about her home life, kind of like me. Maybe that's why I liked her so much.

"Yep. Everything is fine. Later, Tater." She walked out of the room, leaving me alone with my musty dress. I got the feeling her parents were strict, way stricter than Tamara. I felt kind of bad for her. Lynn was a little taller than me and maybe a little heavier. She often got picked on because she wore frosted eyeshadow every day of her life and not much else as far as makeup, but she was kindhearted and usually easy going. I loved her oversized t-shirts and collection of neon-colored tights, even if her outfits never matched.

I was reading too much into her leaving. I had a friend, and that was all that mattered. She never let on there was any kind of problem being here when we took the sparkly eyeballs out of the packaging and scattered them around the sideboard and on the various tables in the living room.

I hoped she'd be able to come back. It wouldn't be the same without her. I had to get this dress on, and the zipper didn't want to work. It had worked just fine last night. I could have asked Tamara to help me—she'd loved the faux-mother bonding crap—but I didn't. When we were downstairs earlier, I thought I heard her talking to someone in her office, but the door had been closed, and I got a feeling that she didn't want me to know who was in there. Definitely a guy, though.

I shimmied into the dress and zipped it up as far as it would go. I needed another pair of hands. A ghostly pair. I opened my bedroom door and stepped into the hallway.

"Psst... Joey? I need your help."

As smooth as he has ever moved, Joey stepped out of the wall, put his hand to his chest and asked, "*Moi*? Really?"

"I need your help with this dress, and I don't want to bother Tamara. Hey, any idea who is in there with her? She's been in that room for half an hour."

Joey was dying to tell me. "The caterers are answering the door for her, but they are not happy about it. You'll never believe who came. He is *so* dreamy! I don't think you can guess. I should make you guess, though, for being such a..."

"Will you just tell me?"

He crossed his arms to show off his muscular arms. He looked good in his fitted sailor costume. I quickly tucked that thought far away. He didn't seem to notice.

"I know exactly who's in there, but I'm not telling you. I have no reason to do so. You act like I'm your pet. You can't just snap your fingers and expect me to show up."

I stomped my foot, but he was holding out. "Joey, for

goodness sake, just tell me. If you tell me, I'll let you help me with my costume." I'd barely gotten the suggestion out of my mouth when he clapped his luminous hands delightfully.

"It's a deal, bestie, but you have to invite me into your room."

We paused outside my bedroom door, and he just hovered there. He was so excited he was glowing like a giant firefly. "All right, let's get your glare under control, please. You are only allowed to come in this one time, and why the invite? It's not like you're a vampire. Are you?"

"Oh, girl. You are a dumb-dumb. No, I'm not a vampire. But I do have to observe boundaries, and you have set plenty. So, can I come in or not?"

He stood there with his hand on his hip expectantly, and I said, "Okay, but like I said, just this one…"

Joey was in my room, sitting on my bed and criticizing the costume jewelry I'd selected. "Um, no way."

"Quinton Lowell from *Ghost Travelers* is in her office. He used to be with *Ghost Hunters,* but that was a long time ago. That's who's down there. Can you believe it? He is her ex, and boy is he a piece of work. Such naughty thoughts, and all the time. I think he regrets losing her, though. Do you think they'll get back together?"

"Who?" I asked. He gave me a crazy look and pulled back again with his hand on his chest.

"Don't tell me you don't know who Quinton Lowell is, Chloe boo? Oh, my God! What is wrong with this generation? The nineties were a much happier time."

"Enlighten me," I said as I tugged at the zipper. "And help me!"

"Grab a wire hanger and get to it. There's making a fashionably late entrance, and then there's just rude. "

"What? Are you going to beat me with it, like that stupid movie you made me watch?"

He tilted his head. "A wire hanger, ma'am. Grab one. I'm saving my energy for my big moment so I can't do it, but it's not hard."

"Quinton Lowell is the number one hottest paranormal investigator in the industry. I mean, how could you not know who he is? Who knew your Aunt Tamara was so connected?" He gave an exaggerated wink and drew his legs up on my bed. "I think they have a past."

I walked to the closet and grabbed a wire hanger. "Yuck. The less I know, the better. And she's not my aunt."

"Okay, sure."

I waved the flimsy hanger at him. "What am I supposed to do with this thing?"

"Use it to pull the zipper up, genius. Slide the hook into the zipper tab and tug it up. Gently. But don't stab yourself. Geesh. Who knew you were so curvy? You go, girl."

Standing in front of the vanity mirror, I did as he suggested and tugged the zipper up. To my shock, it zipped up like a breeze. Yesterday I had thought I looked okay, but I wasn't feeling very confident now. Maybe this was a bad idea.

"Wow! That's great. Thanks, Joey. You think this is a bit much?"

"Oh, you're so welcome. Look at you, wow! You look amazing!"

"You think so?" I asked as I stared at myself in the mirror. "Really?"

"Really. For realz. Now, fix your hair and find some dangly earrings."

"I don't have any dangly earrings. Except these," I said as I slid open the vanity drawer and showed him my silver skulls.

"Why not? I love them! You can go as a dead beauty queen."

My face must have conveyed my many emotions. Mom hadn't been a beauty queen, not in a legitimate way, but she had been beautiful. And she was dead. "Forget what I said. You look beautiful. If you do a messy bun, and maybe use some of that pink hair spray to highlight a few strands, that will make your eyes really pop. Let's do it!"

"Great! I agree! But I can do a messy bun. Back off, handsy. You're welcome to hang out, but I've got this. Are you sure I look okay?"

"Fantastic! Trey is going to be floored! But hands off the deputy. Tamara wants him, she made that clear," he said as he rolled his eyes. "As if I'd be interested in that small-town wannabe sheriff. But Quinton? He's beautiful!"

"Is he here to help us with the Screamer or the Reaper or whatever?" I asked as I slung my head over and began teasing my dark brown hair. It was the only way to get body into it.

"Chloe, stop that. You need to backcomb it, not tease the hell out of it. You'll damage your beautiful hair. Sit up and I'll show you. I won't touch you. I promise. I know I can be a bit chilly. Pick up a section at the crown. Place the comb about two inches from the scalp and very gently backcomb it. Good! Spray and do it again. It's the best way to get the lift you want. On second thought, not a messy bun, but a sexy ponytail. That's what you need."

"Sure, I'll try anything. Quinton is a paranormal investigator, huh? Good. Maybe he can help us get rid of the lights in the backyard."

He suddenly got very serious. "Chloe, I see all kinds of things. I don't know what's going on here anymore than you do, but something unusual is happening, and you're a part of it. I think it's in your blood. That's what the maid said," he said matter-of-factly as he began to file his nails.

I sat at the vanity and stared at his luminous face in the mirror. "What maid? Another ghost?"

"One of the nice ones. I tried talking to Annie Hensley, but she's terrified of me. She thinks I'm a ghost and I want to hurt her. She's a ghost too! She doesn't know she's dead. Kind of ignorant if you ask me. Not like your mother. She's so smart."

He kept filing away, not even noticing he was breaking my heart. He knew my mother, and I couldn't see her. I decided not to cry about it. Tonight, I was going to live my life. I stared at myself in the mirror. I wasn't big into makeup, but I put a little on and then my jewelry. Joey had been right about the pink hair color. I looked great. I took a selfie, with Joey photo bombing me. You could barely see him, but it was a good picture of the two of us.

"Thanks for the help, Joey. It means a lot."

"Will you stop calling me 'the ghost' now?"

I smiled at him and offered to shake his hand. It froze my fingers, but I did it anyway. "Yes, I will. Thank you for tonight. I guess I better go make my entrance." Those were my words, but my feet would not obey. I didn't want to go down those steps. This had been my idea—wearing this dress, paying homage to the memory of my mom—but now I wasn't so sure.

"Go ahead, Chloe. Make your mom proud. I am sure she will be watching." With Joey's encouragement in my ears, I stepped out of my room and into the hallway. I could hear the party well underway downstairs. The music was pumping, and my school friends were laughing and having a good time. I slowly began to walk down the steps to join the fun. I saw Joey snap his fingers and the music changed to an old nineties song, *I Swear*, I think was the name of it. One of those boy band songs. I was pretty sure my mom had liked this song when she'd been alive. I remembered listening to it.

Everyone stopped what they were doing and watched me make the walk down the stairs. I couldn't help but smile like a crazy person. Trey was in the crowd, and he looked just as shocked as the rest of my school friends. Joey had been right. I looked beautiful in this dress, and I had just the perfect amount of curvaceousness. For the first time in my life, I felt pretty.

Really pretty.

Mom, I wish you were here.

But she wasn't, not really. Those were just words Joey had said to make me feel better.

Tamara was there, though, and even from ten feet away, I could see tears in her eyes. She smiled up at me, her white teeth perfect. Her fuzzy headband shook. She was a cute cat. I think she was trying to tell me something, but I couldn't hear what she was saying because the crowd behind her began cheering and whistling. It was a great feeling. I'd never enjoyed this kind of adulation before. For some reason, I thought of Mom. She must have enjoyed feeling all this love. I could see how it was addictive.

Is that why you did it, Mom?

I didn't know if she heard me. The music screamed now, some Halloween song I'd forgotten the name of. The onlookers, my classmates and neighbors I barely knew, were cheering for me. It wasn't like I was an actual beauty queen. There shouldn't be this much excitement about an odd teenager wearing a dress.

Then I looked behind me.

I wasn't alone walking down the steps.

Joey had appeared now that the Screamer was gone. He was walking behind me, looking totally like a living guy. He wasn't dressed like a slinky, gay sailor but a dead prom date. He wore a black suit, black bow tie, and a sleek black cummerbund, like a model out of a magazine. What was he doing?

"Your feet, Joey," I warned him quietly.

"Oh, shoot," he whispered back. He closed his eyes, and his legs appeared. "This is fun!"

"Be quiet, Joey. Don't talk to anyone. Okay? And don't glow!"

We made it to the bottom step, and the ghost kissed my cheek and disappeared into the crowd as best as he could. He glowed ever so slightly, but not enough for anyone to notice, I hoped.

I saw Trey leave the party. He must have thought Joey was real and I was interested in him. I pushed through the crowd to go to him, but he didn't wait, and he didn't look back.

I was the most beautiful girl at my school, and now I was the loneliest. I sat on the steps and watched the dance. People were everywhere, dancing, laughing, and having a great time. The party was a hit for everyone but me. Even Tamara was on the dance floor, shaking her booty with Quinton. She hadn't even noticed Kevin Patrick had snuck in. He was watching her every move.

The partiers believed Joey, my pretend date, was a real guy, even with his too bright smile and occasionally no legs.

As I sat there feeling sorry for myself, I heard a familiar voice in my head. It only lasted a minute, and then she was gone.

Happy Halloween, Chloe. You look beautiful!

"Mom? Is that you?" I whispered as I wiped tears from my eyes. It had to have been her.

She'd finally come through to let me know she saw me and that she loved me. I wasn't going to sit here and be the most boring person at the party. I decided I would dance with someone, even if it wasn't Trey.

Before I could think, Deputy Patrick was in front of me. "Good evening, young lady. Save me a dance later. I've never danced with a belle before. Or a beauty queen. Dead beauty queen, I'm guessing? I'm a cowboy. Or trying to be."

"Why would you want to dance with me? Trying to make Tamara jealous?" My school friends were whispering around me. They knew Deputy Patrick was a cop, and nobody wanted to hang out with anyone who was connected to the cops. "Where did she go? She was just here."

Did I really want to be seen dancing with a cop? Should I attempt to save any level of coolness I may have left?

"She went back to her office with that ghost hunter movie star. Do they have a history or something? Is that why she brought him here?"

"Better question is, why are you here? No idea about who she knows. She was here a minute ago."

Tamara was an idiot. Even though Deputy Patrick was a cop, he was a handsome guy. Way cuter than that any washed-up D-level celebrity. He looked like an old-fashioned cowboy with, of course, a white cowboy hat, just to make it clear that he was a good guy.

"You'll have to teach me, Deputy. I don't know how."

"Your father never taught you how to dance? And please call me Kevin or Mr. Patrick. I'm not on duty."

"Uh, okay. I don't know my dad. Can we just dance?" I asked with my arms crossed. I was aggravated by his questioning.

"No time like the present. The DJ is playing a decent song. Sure, sure. Just hold on to me and follow my lead. It's easy-peasy. I might step on a foot once in a while, but you'll live."

"Ditto. Let's dance, Kevin."

We twirled into the candlelit party.

19

TAMARA

I paced my tiny office and shook my head at Quinton's confused expression. "What were you thinking, coming here? I just wanted your opinion. I didn't know you were going to come down."

"We've been over this. Can't we just enjoy your party? It seems like quite a crowd. Hey, would you mind if I sold a few books? I've got a whole damn box in my van."

I rubbed my itchy nose, forgetting for a second that I had eyeliner all over it. "Are you joking?"

"I'll be friendly and pretend we're the best of friends. If I sell enough of them, I'll be glad to slip you some cash under the table. Why are you so shocked I'm here? You sent me the address." He spoke with his usual attitude. Nothing had changed in the humility department, I thought.

"I sent my address because I thought you needed it for research, not because I wanted you to come down here. Not that I'm not grateful, but..." The music was bumping in the other room. This isn't how I had expected to spend my Halloween. I really needed to get it together.

"Oh, you're not grateful. You don't want me here. It was a huge cock-up. A big misunderstanding. I can see that now, but I'm here and I have three days off, so you might as well tell me what's up."

Why was I struggling with my emotions? I was moved Quinton would come all the way here from Atlanta to check things out, but it was also unlike him. He wasn't usually the kind of guy who jumped and ran when you called. And we had ended on a bad note.

"Well, I've got a party tonight as you may have gathered from the noise and the dancing, and there's a lot going on, so we'll have to revisit this later. I mean, I know you came a long way, and I appreciate it, but this is kind of a bad time."

He laughed, but it didn't sound happy at all. "You are having a party in a place where you know there's paranormal activity? Are you a genius or what? Just the vibes from this place give me the creeps. So, I'll just blend in with the crowd while you're having a Halloween party, right? Pretend I'm a bonus gift. I won't sell my books or anything. I swear."

I walked to the office door and shook my head. "You always believed you were the bonus gift; that was the problem. Party should be over around midnight or so, and then we can talk. In the meanwhile, you can camp out on the second floor. As you say, keep your eyes peeled. See what you can see. Enjoy the party, but behave. There are a ton of teenage girls here. Hands off. I know you aren't the best at checking IDs."

"Will do, Mom," he said sarcastically. "And that's bull-crap. I never dated an underage chick. Not on purpose."

"Whatever. Chloe's room is off-limits. Her bedroom is on the second floor. Chloe doesn't take kindly to strangers, nor does she let anyone in her room. Believe me when I tell you, there's no wrath like the fury of a cantankerous teenager."

"I still can't believe Tina Louise had a kid. Did you know she had a kid? And when did we all get so old that she could be the mother of a teenager?"

"I have no answers for you. Come on, grab your bag. I have just the room for you." Asking him to stay in a hotel would be wrong. There were no hotels close by, and if he'd come all this way to do me a favor, the least I could do was put him up for a night or two. That didn't mean anything was going to happen.

Who was I kidding? It had been a very long time since the two of us were intimate, and I was sure Quinton had moved on to bigger and blonder things since. He'd always had a weak spot for blondes—dumb ones who believed everything he said.

"This is kind of a catch-all room, but there is a bed in here, and I know for a fact the sheets are clean. As far as I know, nothing ever happened here, paranormally speaking. Make yourself at home," I said as the music stopped and somebody screamed. I knew that scream. Quinton dropped his bag on the bed, and the two of us ran into the parlor. The DJ, a young guy not much older than Chloe—a friend of Lynn's she suggested for this gig—stepped out to greet me. He had a big grin on his face.

"Hey! Look who it is! Our hostess with the mostest, and

if I'm not mistaken, this is Quinton Lowell of *Ghost Travelers*. Let the screaming begin!" He tapped his computer keyboard and another scream permeated the room, then the music began again.

A bevy of fans encircled Quinton, and I was quickly forgotten about. I didn't have any shoes on, but the doorbell was ringing. I opened the front door and was amazed. Linda Blabbermouth the neighbor was at the door with a mannequin's head under her arm. She was dressed as Marie Antoinette, a bloody line around her neck. If she was Marie Antoinette with her head chopped off, why was she carrying an extra head around?

"Do you get it? Tell me you get it," she said through bright pink lips.

"Hi, Linda. I'm thinking Marie Antoinette, but the extra head is throwing me off," I told her cheerfully.

"Almost right. I am Marie Antoinette's twin sister." She screamed with delight and hugged my neck as if we were the best of friends.

"Great costume. Come on in. We've got quite the party going. Quinton Lowell is here from *Ghost Travelers*, too," I added, hoping that would distract her.

"Who is that? I've never heard of *Ghost Travelers*. Is that one of them paranormal folks? Maybe I should talk to him about my abilities. They've been getting out of control recently. Oh, dear, I think I'm picking up something now." She squinted and contorted her face as if she were getting some sort of message.

"Oh, really?" I asked as the crazy neighbor took a few steps inside. "There are many ghosts here at the Ridaught Plantation. I think we'll see some tonight."

I barely noticed her miniature husband behind her. He couldn't have been more than five foot two. The diminutive fellow was dressed in a matching costume. I assumed he was dressed as King Louis, the guy who also got his head chopped off. I noticed he didn't have a head under his arm, but his cheeks were bright red as if he'd had a little nip already. I didn't blame him if he had. If I lived with Linda Blabbermouth, I would need a drink too.

I couldn't remember his name. "Hey, sir. Your costume is great. I think the party will get a hoot out of seeing you. Would you mind playing host for me for a few seconds? I left my shoes in the other room."

"Oh, no, I don't mind at all. Come on, King Louis. We will be a welcoming party. Straighten up, honey. Throw those shoulders back. You know, Robbie used to play football for USL? It's been a while, but he was so buff back in those days. I swear, you look positively short, and you've got heels on." She was right, he did have heels on, vintage retro French shoes. Poor Louie, I mean Robbie, had little choice about what he was wearing, and he didn't seem happy about it.

"Hi, I am Tamara. I don't think we've been introduced. Robbie, is it? Would you prefer I call you King Louis tonight?"

"Robert. Linda calls me Robbie, but my name is Robert," he said in a flat voice as if he were some sort of robot. He barely moved his neck, and it was kind of stiff-looking, but it could've been all the ruffles he was wearing.

"Thank you, Robert. You and Linda look fabulous. Feel free to grab some snacks, and there's a bar right over there..."

Before I could get the words out of my mouth, Robert was gone leaving Linda to hold her own head. The doorbell rang, and I thanked Linda again as I hurried off to find my shoes and head to the kitchen to answer the caterer's questions.

Everything looked great. Heather wasn't having any major issues, just spiked punch, which she quickly replaced. Things were going great on the food front.

I hoped the Screamer stayed away. What was that DJ thinking? Come to think of it, the scream didn't sound very much like the scream we'd heard; it was more Hollywood. The real scream had been straight out of another dimension. I slid my feet into the cute leopard print shoes I'd purchased for this outfit.

Time to really get this party started. In a quiet voice, I asked Joey if he was around, but he didn't answer. I assumed he was hanging back somewhere, watching everything with amusement. He'd already made his grand entrance and was probably hiding out now to re-up his energy. I didn't worry about him scaring people on purpose. Joey wasn't that kind of ghost. I was kind of surprised he hadn't sported his sailor costume when he came down the stairs. It was really sweet of him to escort Chloe. Maybe they'd finally decided to be friends. Tina Louise would have been very proud to see Chloe's arrival.

"Okay, Tamara. You can't hide in your room. This was your idea, remember?" With one last look in the mirror, I smiled at myself to make sure there was no lipstick on my teeth. Time to go see Deputy Patrick. The dress was a little short and the headband was probably not very cool, but I felt cute, and that was all that mattered. I've never been one to go in for scary costumes.

"Tina Louise, you would have been proud of your baby tonight. Chloe looked like a true starlet."

Not that Tina Louise had ever been a beauty queen, not to my knowledge, but she'd been a rock star in her day amongst our crowd. Chloe was drop-dead gorgeous, with a figure I hardly recognized.

"I'm trying, TL. If you can help us out with the party, that would be great."

Suddenly, an image began to form in the mirror. Not my image, either.

And not Tina Louise.

I saw the faint image of a woman in a white uniform. Her face was in shadow at first, but it became clearer as I stared. She had dark circles under her eyes, and her dirty-blonde hair was in a bun. The white uniform was dingy, like she had crawled out of the ground. Her eyes were wide, and so was her mouth.

She screamed, and I recognized the sound. Annie Hensley wasn't running from the Screamer. She *was* the Screamer, and there was a reason for the anger and fear she was trying to convey.

When the scream ended, I heard her whisper as if her lips were right next to my ear.

"He's coming!"

CHLOE

To Tamara's surprise, the party began to fade around eleven o'clock. I'd expected that. Most of the kids from my school had other parties to go to, ones that provided booze. It didn't surprise me there were a lot of shenanigans going on in Crystal Springs tonight, none of which parents or law enforcement knew anything about.

It was great that so many people had come from the high school, but I still failed to make many connections. It was cool that Lynn showed up eventually and brought Trey back with her. He acted pouty, but I guess I liked that in a guy because I was sure glad to see him. Lynn wasn't wearing a costume, but Trey wore a mummy t-shirt he'd pinned with random strips of gauze.

At least the guy had tried. He had even gone so far as to wear white pants and tennis shoes. At some point during the night, we ransacked my medicine cabinet and found more gauze bandages to wrap around his head, but it didn't do much to make him look more like a mummy. We slow danced a few times, which was kind of nice. He'd seen Joey come down the stairs with me and admitted it pissed him off, but he got over it. I assured him Joey was just a family friend and nobody I was interested in. I didn't mention he was dead. I'd never slow danced with anyone before tonight, and I danced quite a few times. What was more humorous was watching Kevin and that Quinton guy vying for Tamara's affection. She hustled between them in her leopard-print high heels like a busy queen bee. At least she'd lined up some potential buyers. I hoped she nailed one.

She was doing her dead-level best to make our family look normal, but we were anything but. Happily, at least for her, she made the connections she wanted and got some appointments out of the party. Reality struck me as I undressed. One day all of this would be mine. Trey hinted about heading over to Black Snake Creek, but something about that place gave me the creeps. It was dark out, and there were no lights. There were sure to be tons of teenagers making out or doing whatever it was teenagers did on Halloween night.

I was feeling weak, and for some reason, I wanted to stay close to home. I didn't think we'd ever get rid of Linda Blabbermouth. I picked that name up from Tamara, and it was hard to not call her that to her face. Linda didn't want to go home, but we slowly walked her toward the door.

"Your family has such an interesting history, Chloe. Did you know the builder of this house, or the original house, well, he murdered his wife and his daughters all on the same night? Isn't that creepy? And then there was the case of that runaway coach who was run off the road here and everyone in it died. Oh, and then there's..."

Tamara coughed as if to say excuse me, but Linda wasn't listening. Thankfully, Kevin walked up and offered to help Linda carry her head home since her husband had made tracks back to their residence an hour before.

As I said goodbye to Trey, he surprised me by leaning in for a kiss. Tamara was watching us, and I didn't feel comfortable planting one on him in front of her. I'm sure Tamara knew Trey and I had kissed already, but it seemed weird to do it in front of her.

"Bye, Trey!" I said as I hurried up the steps to my room. Cups and plates weren't littered everywhere, thanks to the catering company that had kept it all under control. There wasn't much to do except blow out the candles and call it a day. I would be happy to hit the hay, only I was pretty sure it would be hours before I went to sleep. I couldn't believe how much I danced and how much fun I had. I couldn't remember the last time I had laughed so hard my face hurt. Joey had behaved himself, appearing only that once. I guess the quick appearance had worn him out, but my classmates had seen him, and they all wanted to know his name. I pretended I didn't know, which pissed them off, but I thought it was hilarious. Imagine, crushing on a ghost.

I had barely changed my clothes when I heard a light tap on my door. I immediately began to pray, which was weird because I wasn't the most religious person on the planet. Not by a long shot.

"Please don't let that be Joey. Please, please, please. I am exhausted." I glanced at the clock. It was almost midnight. For some reason, just observing the hands of the clock about to move to the witching hour caused a shiver to go up my spine. Worse would be if it was a living person tapping on my door, like the investigator dude. It was only Tamara. Her cat eyeliner was smeared and her hair was sagging, but she'd changed her clothes too and was clearly getting ready to hit the sack.

Hopefully by herself. The idea of someone having sex under the same roof was kind of gross.

"Hey, Chloe!" Uh-oh, she sounds a little tipsy. "I know it's late, but I just wanted to say thank you for all you did tonight. Did you have a good time?"

"Yes. It was great. I think everyone had a good time. Well, catch you in the morning." I started to close the door, but Tamara wanted to talk.

"Listen, about Quinton." She slurred her words slightly and put her finger to her lips. Was she asking me to keep quiet? Was she hammered?

"Hey, you don't have to explain yourself to me. I understand how things work with adults. A little birdie told me you guys used to go out. I have to say, I think your friend isn't nearly as hot as Kevin."

"Oh, God! We are not having this conversation. We are not together! I swear it's the truth! He came because I sent him the pictures of that silver and told him about the Screamer. Do you know what I found out? That Screamer is the nurse, Annie Hensley. She screamed at me from the mirror tonight. I almost pissed my pants. I think we need to help her. Or I need to help her. Is this hall wobbling?"

I thought about asking her in. She looked as if she might topple over at any minute, but I was ready to hit the sack. I liked Tamara and all, but we were never going to be besties. Tamara did not deserve my indifference, but I was so tired I could barely keep my eyes open. Unlike most teenagers, I wasn't a natural night owl.

"I just wanted to let you know I did not invite Quinton here. He just kind of showed up."

"Okay, then. Do you need help getting back to your room? I don't mean this in a negative way, but you're kind of sauced, Tam."

Before we could get to arguing about calling her Tam, there was a loud knock on the front door. Not once or twice, but three solid knocks. The knocks were so thunderous I worried the house would fall in. Tamara was instantly sober, and I was wide awake. The two of us quietly traveled downstairs to find out who in the world was banging on the door at midnight. The party had broken up, and the caterers were gone. The DJ had been the first to leave. I heard he had a gig down by Black Snake Creek.

As Tamara's hand reached for the doorknob, I experienced major panic. I couldn't say why, but later I would think about this moment and concluded it was my primal spiritual being warning me. Watching Tamara's hand reach for the doorknob was like watching a scary movie, only in slow motion. I knew something horrible was coming, but I did not know how to stop it. I choked out a whimper as the hammering suddenly resumed.

Tamara pulled her hand away, and she was looking over my shoulder. Joey raced up behind us. The ghost had no legs, and he was sporting a Hello Kitty do-rag, which was clearly mine. He was also wearing shorts that were far too tight for him and a fitted pink T-shirt, and he was clutching a stuffed rabbit.

I had been wondering where my stuffed rabbit Marco had got to.

"What is going on? Why are you so loud? Some of us need our beauty sleep."

As the door squeaked open, the three of us watched the horrifying scene unfold before us. There were ghosts in the front yard. Not cut-up sheets hanging from the trees or the little inflatable ghosts we had anchored near the bird fountain. These were actual ghosts, the dead, in our yard, in varying degrees of decomposition.

Leading the pack was the lady in white. That had to be the nurse Tamara had been telling me about. As the door remained open, the three of us were frozen in our tracks. The blood-covered nurse screamed at us, and it practically blew my hair back. Then Joey screamed beside me. Tamara and I joined in the hysterical chorus.

"Shut the door! Shut the door!" I yelled since Tamara appeared to be frozen to the spot. I slammed it shut and locked it, but no sooner had I turned then Joey took off, his silly image disappearing into the stairs. Quinton came running out of one of the guestrooms.

"What is it? What the hell is going on? Who is doing that screaming?"

"The Screamer! It's Annie Hensley, and she's not alone! Do something, Quinton!" Tamara demanded, completely sober now.

"What? Is this a joke?"

I could hardly get involved in this argument because there were footsteps on the front porch. Not one pair, but at least half a dozen people were clamoring onto the steps and the wraparound porch. If I dared to look out one of the windows, I believed I would see a face pressed against the glass. I wasn't going to look because that was the last thing I wanted to see.

"What do we do? What do we do?" I muttered as Tamara and Quinton argued in the foyer. I wasn't going to wait for those yo-yos. I took off upstairs. All I could think about was getting to my room. At least there, I knew I would have some level of protection. As I cleared the landing, I could see Joey hovering outside it.

"Please let me in! Please let me in!" He jumped up and down as he clutched Marco bunny. His luminosity faded in and out. I felt sorry for him and agreed.

"Wait a minute. If I let you in here, can the rest of them come in?" He shook his head, his eyes practically bouncing around in his head.

I didn't wait for Tamara and Quinton to join us. Joey hovered in the corner of my room, acting as if he couldn't breathe. As I dug out my treasure box of paranormal goodies, I reminded him he already couldn't breathe.

"You have to dim your light, Chloe! For the love of everything, you have to dim it down! They can see us!"

"I don't know how," I confessed as I reached for the black stones and essential oils. "I don't know how!"

"Well, figure it out, sister, because they are coming, and there are so many of them. It's a ghost apocalypse! I told you to dim your light. Dim it now!"

I stared at him, dumbfounded as he began to flicker in and out of view. And then we heard running in the hallway.

Joey yelped once before he faded.

TAMARA

"Do something, Quinton! We've got to stop this!" As I spoke, there was banging on the front door.

"You're bullshitting me, Tamara. Total bullshit! I get it. You and the cop are pulling my leg, but this isn't funny." He was shouting at me because of the loudness of the banging. Then it suddenly stopped. I stared at him as if he had two heads.

"Take a look, idiot!"

He sighed deeply and walked to the front door like he was going to open it. I meant to look from the window, not open the door. "No!" I shouted in protest, but he opened the door anyway, and to my surprise, there wasn't a soul on the porch. Ghostly sheets hung from the trees near the front door and bounced around in the wind, but there wasn't anything to see. No Annie Hensley, and no crowd of dead folks trying to get into the Ridaught Plantation.

Quinton slammed the door, and immediately there was a knock. Quinton frowned at me, but I shrugged. I had no way of knowing who the hell had banged on the door. They weren't there a few seconds ago.

Quinton swore as he opened the door again, but he'd barely gotten it open before he slammed it again. "Holy hell!" With that, he took off, leaving me standing alone in the foyer. The banging on the front door continued.

"Hey! Where are you going?" I asked. The activity on the porch got quiet again, and I could finally move again. To my surprise, Quinton came back out of the guestroom with his bag in his hand.

"Where are you going?" I asked in disbelief.

"You've got a problem, Tamara. I can't help you."

I gasped at his declaration. "You are an investigator, Quinton. You can't just run away. Help me figure this out."

He shook his head and avoided making eye contact. "I'm not going to lie to you. I'm out of my element with all this. Good luck, Tamara."

"What?" I stupidly asked as I followed him out the kitchen door. It closed with a slam. "What are you doing?" I demanded, but he kept walking.

There was no more banging or footsteps on the front porch, but I didn't trust the quiet. I didn't trust it at all.

I heard Quinton's van crank up and spin out of the driveway.

The sonofabitch had left us high and dry. I had to get to Chloe.

I hurried up the steps and burst into her room. She was pacing, and Joey was nowhere to be seen.

"What's going on, Tamara? Where is Quinton?"

"Gone. He split. We have to do this on our own, Chloe. Are you okay? And Joey?"

"What do you mean, gone?" Chloe's eyes widened, and she raced to the window to look outside. "Oh, my God! He *is* gone! What the hell? Tamara, look at this. Look!"

I pulled the curtain back and stood beside her. There were dim lights bouncing all over the yard. The dead were everywhere. The house began to shake as if an earthquake were trembling beneath it. Everything inside me told me to run—take Chloe and run—but how could I do that? This was Chloe's legacy and her home.

"We're not leaving, Chloe. I know what we have to do. Do you trust me?"

The teenager's eyes were full of unshed tears. "I don't know, Tamara. I don't know! I don't trust anyone."

Her confession hurt my heart, but it was an honest answer. "You can trust me, Chloe. We don't need Quinton's help. We can put an end to this. Annie Hensley wants our help. *Your* help. We have to go back down there. We have to help her."

"Help her how? I'm not going back down there!" Chloe said as she stepped away from the curtain.

The trembling ended, but now the windows were rattling gently. The pounding on the door continued.

"If you don't, they'll come inside. Eventually, they will come inside. We have to help her. She's not going away," I said firmly. "You have to help her. Trust me this once. Just once, Chloe."

To my surprise, she took my hand, and we headed back downstairs. In my mind, it was all coming together—how we could help Annie. She was the strongest of the unhappy dead here. She'd been screaming for our attention for weeks. If we could help her, we might be able to put everyone to rest, at least for a while. Until Chloe could get a handle on her abilities.

And me.

I'd been hiding them for too long. It was me Annie had reached out to, but it was Chloe's light that had drawn her here.

"I'm going to open the door, Chloe. She's not going to hurt us. She just wants your help. Our help. We can do this. We have to do this because this is our house. We have to take a stand. No running away from our home—your home. Trust me, Chloe. Please say you trust me."

The doorknob began to rattle, and Chloe stared at it. In a voice like steel, she agreed. "Okay, I'll try."

With shaking fingers and a stomach that felt like an upturned bowl of Jell-O, I reached for the doorknob. It immediately stopped moving. "I'm opening the door, but you can't come in. You cannot come in, Annie. We're only speaking to Annie."

Without much effort, the door swung open. There was no one there—that I could see anyway. Then I saw the shimmering outline of someone who looked like a female. Annie?

That was not the case for Chloe. By the expression on her face, I knew she was seeing the nurse in vibrant, horrible color.

"Um, Tamara?"

"Do you see her, Chloe?"

She nodded slowly. "She's the nurse, she's bleeding. Her head is bleeding. Oh, God, I can't do this."

"You *can* do it. I'm here with you. Hold my hand. I'm right here."

"She's just staring at me, moaning. I don't know how to do this. And there are more coming!"

As she said that, I noticed there were amber-colored lights hovering at the end of the driveway. They'd come up to the house earlier but had wandered away. They were coming back now.

"Don't panic. Talk to her. Ask her if her name is Annie."

"Annie?" Chloe said as she wobbled on her feet. "Yes, that's her name. She's looking for Marge. Or Maggie. Oh, crap. She's getting aggravated with me."

I could hear faint buzzing in my ears, but nothing specific. "Annie, please be patient with us. We're trying to help you. You'll have to talk louder."

"Marjorie! That's the name. She is looking for Marjorie."

I squeezed Chloe's hand. I could feel her trembling, and the lights were getting closer. We didn't have much time left. "Annie, Marjorie isn't here. She doesn't come here anymore. She's gone, Annie." I wasn't sure that was true. How could I know where Marjorie was or wasn't? But it felt right. Annie needed to know Marjorie wasn't her responsibility anymore.

Suddenly an anguished face began to materialize in front of us. Her mouth twisted in a silent scream, then she vanished like smoke on the wind.

Chloe's hands covered her ears, and she began to cry. "Make her stop!"

I called on my past experience. During some of my past paranormal investigations, I had worked with psychics. They always talked about opening doors for the dead and helping them move on. That had to be it. I wasn't a medium like Chloe, but I felt sure we could do this. Together.

"Listen to me, Chloe. We've got to show Annie a door. A door of light."

"What are you talking about?"

"We have to hurry. I want you to visualize a door, okay? Right next to Annie. I'm going to talk to her, and you tell me what she says. I can feel her and see her a little, but I can't hear her."

"Okay, but hurry!"

"Annie, Marjorie is safe. She's waiting for you on the other side of that door. Do you see the door?"

Chloe shook her head. "I'm showing it to her, but she's worried about Marjorie. She says he will hurt her if he finds her. She can't leave Marjorie."

"Who, Annie? Who will hurt Marjorie? Did he hurt you?"

"She says, yes. He hurt her. Paul, she knew him from work. He will come back. He's come back before!" Chloe's pitch rose as she connected with the spirit.

"No, Annie. He's gone now. We will make sure everyone knows what happened to you. We promise. Please, go to Marjorie. She's waiting for you. We're opening the door now, and you have to walk through. Only good things are on the other side of that door. You've done your job, Annie. You took care of Marjorie. She's safe, and she's waiting." The lights were getting closer; we were about to be inundated with ghosts. I wasn't ready, and neither was Chloe.

Chloe gasped as she whispered, "She's going, Tamara! She's going through the door! She's gone! Oh, my God!

She's gone!" Even as she said the words, I felt a noticeable dip in the atmosphere.

"Close the door, Chloe! Close it! See it and close it!"

Weeping, the teenager closed her eyes and bowed her head. Her visualization must have worked because the yard became still. Only a few lights remained.

"Now, one last thing. I want you to visualize the light that's around you. See it, Chloe. See the light. What color is it?"

"Pink," she said without hesitation as she continued to cry.

"That's good, honey. Now see that light dimming. See it fading. Turn it off, Chloe. Shut it down. Dim your light. You can do it."

"I'm trying," she whispered as the remaining lights flickered and vanished. I slammed the door shut, and Chloe fell into my arms.

We cried together as I stroked her hair and told her everything would be all right. There was no way I could know that, but I sure hoped.

I wanted it to be true. With all my heart, I wanted it to be true.

Maybe it would be.

EPILOGUE

TAMARA

"I can't believe they are finally bringing the show back. Oh, and look, it's Quinton. Change the channel, please. I can't stand to watch his sorry self. Ghost hunter, my ass." Joey's hand reached for the popcorn bowl and tossed a few buttery kernels into his open mouth. Naturally, the popcorn fell right through his faintly luminous image and bounced off the back of the couch. I clamped my lips together to prevent myself from laughing at his silliness. I think he did things like that for attention. He was always trying to shock me.

But I laughed along with him. You had to pick your moments with Joey. After all we'd been through, the last thing I wanted was to hurt his feelings by pointing out he would never eat popcorn again.

I reached for the remote to change the channel when music began playing upstairs. Slow, sulky music. I couldn't quite hear the lyrics, but I was pretty sure they were about the angstinesss of teenage love. I cocked my head toward the ceiling, but it was impossible to hear any conversation.

I wasn't sure if that was good or bad. Trey and Chloe were up there, along with Chloe's new friend Lynn. If it had been just the two lovebirds by themselves, I would have insisted they hang out downstairs, but surely, I had nothing to worry about.

Joey's ears perked up too. "Want me to go take a look?"

It was my turn to reach for the popcorn. "No. Give the kids their privacy. Lynn's up there too."

"Which means?" Joey asked with his trademark cocked eyebrow.

"It means you have to have privacy to make out."

Joey sighed as if I were the stupidest woman in the world. Maybe I was.

"Oh, sweetie. You're so behind the times."

I frowned as I tucked the blanket around my legs. I loved Joey, but he tended to take all the warmth out of the air when he got close.

"Fine. Take a peek, but don't let her see you."

He was gone for the show's intro but reappeared quickly. "That's a sad trio. They're actually studying."

"See?" I answered, feeling renewed confidence in my initial diagnosis. "I told you so."

"You're so stupid, Tamara. Of course, they're kissing. Lynn is surfing the internet, posting crap on Faceworld, and nobody is studying a damn thing. It's all pretty normal."

"You lie," I said as I swatted his semi-transparent hand from the popcorn bowl.

"I never lie, you know that. They aren't doing anything dirty. Calm down."

I flung popcorn at him, then turned to another paranormal show and turned the volume up. I'd give them a few minutes, and then I'd take Chloe's laundry up. It was only a t-shirt and some shorts, but it was enough to give me an excuse to peek in on them. Maybe I'd bring up some popcorn too. Yeah, that's what I'd do. I'd been meaning to watch this new show about a medium who went to famous places and solved cold cases. How apropos. Joey and I were riveted to the television as the medium began her work at the Hopkins House. I'd heard of the place, but I'd never been there. Maybe I'd make a road trip one day.

The commercials appeared rather quickly. I muted the remote and was relieved to hear the music upstairs had changed to something more upbeat. Joey dusted popcorn off the couch and smiled at me sheepishly.

"This place could use a few passes with the vacuum." He crossed his legs and reclined as if we were really relaxing. It was a strange thing to see, his body disappearing into the couch. He was tired; I could see that from his faded aura. We all were. It had been a crazy month here at the Ridaught Plantation, and it had started the day Joey'd put his head in the oven. I had forgotten about that.

"You never told me why, Joey."

He twisted his lips and then asked, "Why what?"

"Why did you put your head in my oven? Clearly, you were upset about something, and that was before we knew about Chloe's mediumship and the path. Before we knew about all the dead out there."

"Show's back on." He smiled smoothly.

"I'm your friend, right? You should be able to talk to me. I'm worried about you. Tell me why you did it. How can I help you? Do you want to talk about it? I think you should."

He reached over and patted my hand. A freezing sensation crept up my arm. I struggled to remain calm, but I managed it. At least it was only a brief touch.

"I don't know why. I've never been dead before. It just felt like the thing to do."

"Come on. That's bull, and you know it. Tell me the truth."

He twisted his lips thoughtfully. For a moment I believed he would tell me, but he didn't. Sexy music began flowing again upstairs, and I heard the front door open and close. Lynn's noisy car cranked up—I could hear it from the living room couch. That meant two teenagers were alone upstairs. That wasn't happening today.

"Want me to go up again?"

"No. Let me do it. I'll be right back."

By the time I made it up there, the two of them were pretending to study, so I plopped down her laundry and left them alone.

I propped the door open. "Leave it open, please, or study downstairs."

Chloe sighed dismissively as she pretended to read her upside-down textbook. Trey blushed as he scribbled in his notebook. What was he drawing? Little hearts on the page. Oh, brother.

Chloe must really think I was a fool. I'd pretend to be one if it helped her feel normal, but only to a point.

I hurried back to the living room so I wouldn't miss a moment of the new program.

"Do you think he'll give you credit?" I didn't have to ask

what he was talking about. He meant Deputy Kevin Patrick. I'd had coffee with him a few days ago and shared the information I had about Annie's killer, Paul West. He'd quickly located him, and to our surprise, the guy had made a full confession. West had been stealing meds from the patients and selling them. He'd thought Annie was going to the police, and he'd offed her to silence her. Marjorie had been fine, just lost in the woods. She'd died a year after Annie.

"Cripes, that's a terrible story. What did Sexy Cop say about your ghost-busting skills? Is he still investigating the serial killer murders?"

"Kevin didn't want to believe how I came by the information, but that was on him. I know what I saw and what Chloe and I experienced. He didn't say anything about the serial killer, or if there ever was one. You know how he is. Deputy Patrick keeps his cards close to the vest. Kind of like someone else I know."

"Hm. Well, all's well that ends well." We watched television for a little while longer. When the commercials began to roll, I muted it. Time to go back upstairs and check on Chloe and Trey.

"I made a major decision, Joey. I'm going to write a ghost story. I plan on telling Annie's story."

Joey snatched the edge of the blanket away from me as he said, "Really? You've abandoned the romance novel?"

"Yep. My first novel will be a ghost story. Maybe the second one, too. I have so many ideas."

"It's just as well, sweetie." He smirked as he nodded at the remote. "I don't think you have the knack for shirt-ripping romance. Ghost stories? Yeah, you can do those. They're back. Turn it up, please."

"Thanks for the vote of confidence, bestie."

He touched me again with his icy fingers. "I've always got your back, Jack. Now pipe down. I think this medium is legit. Not as legit as our Chloe, though."

The cicadas clicked outside, music played above us, and my ghostly best friend kept stealing the popcorn. Despite her creaking floorboards and haunted grounds, the Ridaught Plantation felt like home.

We were all home at last.

The End

Tamara's story continues with *Always Dead*, book two in the Welcome To Dead House series, coming soon to Amazon and Kindle Unlimited.

THE SEVEN SISTERS COTTONWOOD
OMNIBUS EDITION

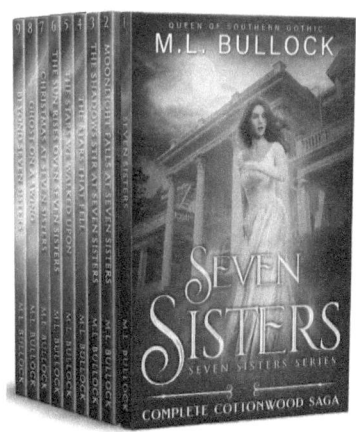

Available now at Amazon and through Kindle Unlimited.

Updated & Expanded FULL Omnibus version for Feb 2020!

The Seven Sisters Ultimate Cottonwood Saga, including two bonus stories.

When historian Carrie Jo Jardine accepted her dream job as the chief historian at Seven Sisters in Mobile, Alabama, she had no idea what she would encounter.

The moldering old plantation housed more than a few boxes of antebellum artifacts and forgotten oil paintings.

Secrets lived there--and they demanded to be set free.

When young, wealthy Ashland Stuart offered Carrie Jo the job, he had no idea that she had a secret of her own.

An unexpected accident takes Carrie Jo back in time as a witness to life at the plantation over 150 years ago.

An impassioned plea from Ashland puts Carrie Jo in a precarious position as the two work together to find young and beautiful missing heiress Calpurnia Cottonwood.

A collection of journals and a series of dreams give Carrie Jo all the clues she needs to find the missing girl, but both a present-day danger and one from the past try to stop her.

Will Carrie Jo solve the mystery of the house *or will she go missing forever herself?*

Grab your copy today!

AUTHOR'S NOTE

Thank you so much for reading *Never Dead*. It feels so good to begin a spooky new journey with fresh faces. I look forward to getting to know Tamara, Joey, and Chloe, and of course, all the ghosts who find their way to the Ridaught Plantation. I have so many stories I want to tell you. Please stick around!

If this is the first book of mine you've read, please consider moving on to another one of my series. *Seven Sisters* is a spooky journey back in time to haunted Mobile, Alabama. If you prefer a book featuring larger casts and in-depth paranormal investigation, check out the *Gulf Coast Paranormal Series*.

Want to be notified when my next book releases? Click here.

Want to follow me on social media and see my writing progress? Eager to get peeks of my daily life and take a peek at my embarrassingly extensive planner collection? I have you covered.

Follow me here: Facebook - Twitter – Instagram – Website

Thank you so much for purchasing this book and for following me. If you enjoyed it, please consider leaving a review or recommending it to a friend.

Thank you again for your support!

M.L. Bullock

MEET THE AUTHOR

Author of the best-selling *Seven Sisters* series and the *Gulf Coast Paranormal* series, M.L. Bullock has been storytelling since she was a child. A student of archaeology, she loves weaving stories that feature local Alabama legends. She currently lives on the Gulf Coast with her family but frequently travels to explore the southern states she loves so much. When she's not writing, she enjoys the odd paranormal investigation. The odder, the better.

Connect with M.L. Bullock on Facebook. To receive updates on her latest releases, visit her website at M.L. Bullock and subscribe to her mailing list. You can also contact her at authormlbullock@gmail.com.

OTHER BOOKS BY M.L. BULLOCK

Seven Sisters: The Cottonwood Saga

The Idlewood Collection: The Complete Idlewood Series

Beyond Seven Sisters

The Desert Queen Collection: The Complete Series

The Hauntings of Sugar Hill

Lost Camelot